F*Ck Yeah

Knox Academy - ~~Term Two~~ 2.5 Easter Break

By Crystal North & Jaye Pratt

First Edition.
Cover art by Soxational Cover Art
Formatting by Formatting and Design by Jaye.
Editing by CB Editing Services

Dedication

This book is STILL not dedicated to Hannah.

Blurb

Tragedy draws Amelie back to Australia once again, but this time she's not alone. It's been decided that she needs a break, and what better way to do that then with Kalen in her homeland? You can guarantee that with Fairy Bread, kangaroos, mosquitos, and the youngest Knox brother, chaos will ensue. Add in even more secrets, lies and deceit, and Amelie's in for one hell of a ride. Because what's a holiday without a little drama?

Meanwhile, where is Baxter Branson? Who is the raven haired beauty that has snagged his attention? And is he really capable of feelings and friendships?

This novella follows Amelie and Baxter Branson on their Easter Break from Knox Academy. After all the drama of term 2, some much needed rest and relaxation is in order, don't you think? Read F*ck Yeah, book 2.5 of the gripping Knox Academy Reverse Harem series now.

Chapter One

Amelie

"Do not stand by my grave and weep…" the priest or minister or whatever he's called drones on, reciting some famous death poem or other.

Easier said than done.

I thought I'd be immune to today. Numb. But sly tears sneak past my defences and snake their way down my face.

Wordlessly, the guy on my right hands me a tissue and I take it gratefully. I wipe my eyes and pocket the item, knowing that now the water works have started, I'll need it again.

A gentle nudge draws my attention and I look at the guy on my left.

"Amelie, it's time."

He nods toward the white rose in my hand. It symbolises loyalty. Everyone in attendance here today has one, but only *family* will place theirs on top of the coffin.

Stepping forward on shaky legs, I place my rose in the centre of the simple casket. Today's send off isn't a lavish affair. What's the point in spending all that money on a box that sits in the ground to rot? The money will be better spent on the living, for the wake afterwards, back at the house.

Once people have stepped forward to pay their respects, the coffin is lowered. The smooth movement jars against the seizing of my heart. I slip my hand into Kalen's on my right and squeeze. More tears fall. My knees shake. I blink and I'm transported back to that night.

"Onyx, I forgive you, okay?! On, please don't die on me!" *Helpless sobs wrack my entire body and hot angry tears stream down my face.*

"Amelie? Milly? It's time to go," my brother gently calls to me. It's like he's speaking from a great distance but a gentle shake brings me back. "You okay? Are you *crying?*"

I nod.

"You barely even knew the guy," Smalls grumbles under his breath. Kalen hisses at him in warning.

I look at Kalen, understanding and pain reflected back at me.

"Yeah, sorry. I'm here." I wipe my face again but a moment later it's wet once more. The tears won't seem to stop, even though I make no sound. Stupid. Just another part of me that's broken. Like —

"Okay. Do you want to ride to the wake with us or…"

"You guys go," I say to him and Smalls. "I'll ride with Kalen and see you there."

They give Kalen a sideways look, unsure about leaving me with him. I don't blame them, the flight only got in this morning so there wasn't much time for pleasantries before we all had to get ready for the funeral.

"Why the fuck would someone call it a funeral? The word starts with FUN," Kalen points out. I agree with him. It's all bullshit.

"Whoever came up with that one was a stupid arsehole."

This time, Aadi and Smalls give *me* the sideways look.

"*Arsehole*, Milly, really?" My brother looks unamused.

"What the hell happened to you?" Smalls demands.

"Kalen rubbed off on me. I *do* live in England now. In the middle of bum fuck Egypt, actually. You're going to have to get used to some Britishisms slipping in."

They both crack weak smiles and step forward to kiss my forehead.

"Love you, sis. It's damn good to see you again, even under shitty circumstances."

"Love you, babygirl."

Kalen's jaw clenches.

"Love you guys too."

They leave and then it's just Kalen and I, standing graveside, alone.

"You know," I say, turning to Kalen. "It's not a competition, Kalen. They loved me first, deal with it."

"Well, I love you most." He pouts.

"Not a competition," I repeat.

"Look around, Amelie. There's *less* competition now. It's just you and me, *babygirl*."

"Ugh. Don't call me that."

"You didn't say that to *him*."

"Smalls has been calling me that almost my entire life. Stop with the jealous act. And your earlier comment was in poor taste," I scold him. And then I sag into his arms, unable to keep the sobs at bay any longer. They echo off the gravestones and my body shakes with the force of them.

"Shh, sis, it's okay."

"D-d-don't let Aadi hear you call m-m-me t-that," I squeeze out between sobs.

"Pah! I'm not scared of him."

"You should be."

"You're telling me. There were some right dodgy types here today. Way worse than The Order."

I nod in agreement. I'll be having words with Smalls about that later. They owe me some answers. "So, why are you crying?"

"Because today could so easily have been for Onyx..."

"But it wasn't. He's f—"

"Do *not* say he's fine, Kalen! He is definitely not fine."

"I know. But he's waiting back home for you. They all are."

"I know but—"

"No buts."

"I'm really worried about Baxter. Will we be doing this all over again when we get home?"

"I know. But I promise that we have the best of The Order searching for him. They'll find him. Alive."

"And when they do, I'll kill him," I vow.

"Atta girl. Now, are we done crying by the grave of some dude you didn't even know? Can we go to the party now?"

"It's called a wake, you asshole."

"I think you mean *arsehole*." He grins and winks at me, then pouts. "That's no fun. I was hoping it would be called something different down under."

"Please don't ever say that again. In fact, don't try to do an Aussie accent again 'cause you'll get your *arse* kicked. And I won't defend you."

"Harsh. We're family. We're supposed to stick together."

"Let's go, Kalen." I shake my head at how incorrigible he is, but I guess his plan worked. I stopped crying, put my Onyx and Baxter demons back in their box, and even managed a joke and a smile.

"I think this is going to be good for me," I tell him.

"What is?"

"This. Being here, in Australia, with you."

"Two whole weeks to live it up, Aussie style?! Fuck yeah! Let's do this!"

Amelie: Are you okay?

Message undelivered

Chapter Two

Baxter

I'm starting to wonder if pressing that emergency SOS button on my phone was a bad idea. It took a while for the memories of the blast to come back to me, but the one thing that was a constant certainty for me was Amelie. I remember that we fought and I walked off, then there was a blast. I came round outside, way too far from the building to have been thrown, propped up against a tree. So I dialled for Grandfather's help.

I knew by activating that damn button – and the attached tracker – that my grandfather would find me swiftly and get me to safety, but I didn't anticipate how stir-crazy I'd find myself going, stuck on his private island.

His doctors say I was injected with some sort of drug, but so far have been unable to identify it. It's bound to be some new synthetic shit, but it's done a real number on me. Weeks later, and I'm still as fragile as I was on day one.

When I find out who's responsible for this, I will *butcher* them. Order rules be damned.

To make matters worse, the old man won't get off my back

about The Order. I just wanted to get away from them all, and yet here he is, ramming their virtues down my throat at every opportunity. He thinks they're wonderful, even though he's practically a ghost within their ranks. They let him get away with that shit because of the reach, connections and money that he has. He wants me to step up and take a more active role. It's driving me crazy.

Not to mention that I can't seem to go anywhere on this godforsaken island without bumping into him and his bloody floozy.

I'm not stupid; I know that woman has been in his life longer than I've been alive. It doesn't matter that my grandmother died twenty years ago and that I can barely remember her, it's an insult to her memory. The day I found out my grandfather had cheated on my grandmother – pretty much from the first day of their marriage – was the day I lost all respect for him outside of the boardroom.

And now he's hassling me to join him in business too. He wants to groom me to take over the vast Branson empire.

Like I give a shit. About any of it.

I just need to heal from the explosion, survive another two weeks here, and then head back to Knox to finish my sentence. I plan to keep my head down and leave anything to do with The Order well alone.

And that includes Amelie. She's one of them now. I tried to save her, but I failed. She'd have been better off dying in that blast. The alternative – selling her sole to The Order – is way worse.

I sigh and firmly lock thoughts of Amelie in a mental box never to be opened again. I don't know what it is about her, but she makes me weak. Unstable. Dangerous.

Though of course, my inner psycho quite likes that. Spilling blood in her honour has been the most fun I've had in years.

No. I need to stop.

Standing, I wince a little, still tender from the blast. It's been almost three weeks and I'm still weak as a baby from whatever shit I was injected with. I had a concussion from the blast and the last thing I remembered was speaking to Amelie—

Fuck it. I can't keep her from my mind. She's well and truly under my skin.

"Ah, here you are. I wondered where you'd been sulking lately. Haven't seen you about." My grandfather grins at me, that woman peering over his shoulder with a sneer on her face, and I scowl at the pair of them. But mostly her.

Reaching for a cigarette, I place it between my lips and light it.

"Not sulking," I say, taking a long drag before exhaling and blowing the smoke in her direction. "Healing."

"Mmm-hmm," Grandfather replies sceptically. The only thing worse than him getting at me about school, business and The Order, is the person he becomes when his mistress is around. I don't like it one bit. "Listen, we have a visitor arriving soon."

"We?"

"Cordelia's granddaughter is coming to stay for a while."

I perk up a little. Fucking with Cordelia is my favourite pastime, and fucking her granddaughter is bound to mess with her head and cause friction between her and my grandfather. Maybe I can fuck her up a little too. Now that Amelie has unleashed my thirst for blood once again, I find myself craving it more than sex.

Unfortunately, my grandfather must see the spark of interest in my eyes because he quickly shuts my plans down.

"No, Baxter. Not this time. Aren't there enough staff members on the island to whet your appetite?" He sighs, like this is just another thing he can chalk up against me in the massive list of ways I disappoint him.

"I've worked my way through them all," I lie. "Twice."

Well, maybe it's only a half lie. I definitely worked my way through the staff over the Christmas holidays. Twice. Maybe he has some new recruits for me now? Not that I've been feeling up to it. But for this granddaughter chick, I could grit my teeth and persevere.

Cordelia tuts like I'm a disgusting creature, but it takes one to know one. Marriage wrecker that she is.

"Charlotte," she snaps. "I mean, Raven, is a good girl. You will stay far away from her Baxter!"

Huh? Is that so? Why doesn't she know her own granddaughter's name? And what sort of name is Raven anyway? If I wasn't so against associating with The Order, I could have put in a call to get more answers. I hate a mystery.

"Or what?" I challenge, blowing more smoke into her face. She coughs, swipes at the air, glares at me.

"Or your grandfather will cut you off."

I bark out a laugh. Of course he will.

"Right." I snort derisively.

"I mean it, Baxter—" Grandfather joins in with the threats. Wow, this must be serious. This chick is either underage or has a platinum pussy. Colour me intrigued. I wonder if her blood runs blue. Will I get to find out?

"As your soul heir, I very much doubt that you're going to cut me off." I turn to sneer at Cordelia. "And your withered choice of fuck toy here is practically prehistoric. She'd give birth to dusty corpse babies if you tried to knock her up and make a new heir."

"Dicky!" Cordelia gasps, affronted by the truth.

"Unless he has some younger bits on the side, now that you've been promoted to main piece."

"Baxter! That is enough!" Now my grandfather has to chastise me in order to save face. Which tells me he probably is boning the staff too. Ugh, that's a grim thought. We've never had the same taste. And I mean, I'm all for Daddy kink, but imagine being told your granddaddy does it better...

I feel sick.

"Baxter! Are you listening? You will be a perfect gentleman when Cordelia's granddaughter arrives. You will stay out of sight as much as possible and when you have to interact with her, you will be on your best behaviour!"

"Or else you'll cut me off? Yeah, yeah."

"No. I won't cut you off Baxter. You're my only family—"

Cordelia coughs.

"You're my blood. But I will call Monty and use a favour to get your sentence at Knox extended," he finishes sadly, like it pains him to have to make such a threat.

Only it's not a threat. I know beyond a shadow of a doubt that my grandfather means every word. And I cannot allow that to happen. Because spending a moment longer than I have to at Knox Academy might just shatter what little of my soul is still intact.

Amelie: Are you okay?

Message undelivered

Amelie: Where are you?

Message undelivered

Amelie: Stop ignoring me!

Message undelivered

Amelie: I thought we were friends…

Message undelivered

Amelie: Well fuck you very much!

Message undelivered

Chapter Three

Amelie

24 hours earlier

"Did anyone ever tell you, you're the human version of a headache?" I despair. Kalen is crazy annoying me. A quick glance at my watch tells me there's still way too many hours of this flight left to go.

"Actually yeah, O says that to me all the time." He grins at me and I can't help but smile. It *is* such an Onyx thing to say. Then my face falls.

"Kalen—"

"Don't 'Kalen' me, he's fine. I promise."

"We shouldn't be doing this. We shouldn't be going away and leaving him."

"You know if he was fit to fly, he'd be here, right?"

"Exactly. If he's not fit to fly, I shouldn't be leaving him! He needs me!" I cry.

It doesn't matter that we've been having this conversation for weeks, the guilt wracks me and tears threaten to spill when I realise I should never have got on this damn plane.

How did Kalen convince me again?

Ah, the sex. The amazing, I'm so relieved your brother didn't die and I can't bear to look at his twin without bursting into tears but I need comfort from someone right now, mind blowing monster cock sex.

"And Smalls? Aadi? Don't they need you right now too?"

"But—"

"But nothing. They would never have asked if they didn't really need you to come."

I know he's right. It's part of the reason why my stomach is in knots. Onyx barely survived the gunshot wound and blow to the head.

I ran, but I soon came to my senses. I was so terrified that he was going to die and that I would lose another person I love, that I bolted to avoid the pain. It didn't work. The not knowing was agony, so I found help and got a lift straight to the hospital.

Onyx ended up in a coma for nine days and kept in for observation another seven after that. He's only been out of hospital a couple of days, but when Smalls called and said that Brenton – a close friend of him and my brother – had died, and begged me to come back for the funeral, what choice did I have?

I took a lot of persuading, and it was only Kalen deciding to come with me – I think at Monty's insistence – that finally made me cave and agree to come. So that's how I came to be stuck on a twenty-hour flight back to Queensland, with the most annoying human known to man. As if that wasn't bad enough, I've had to leave my baby, Mo-Mo, at home with Sawyer. For two weeks. I don't know how I'm going to survive without them all for that length of time. Kalen insists I can survive on chocolate – since we will be spending Easter with my family – and sex. Little does he know there is no way in hell my brother or Smalls will let him sleep in my room. He'll get the guest bedroom. Which is a tiny box of a room, big enough for a child sized bed. Chelsea uses it when her nieces and nephews come to stay.

"Look, sis—" Kalen begins in a weirdly reproachful tone.

"Not your damn sister, Kalen. And my brother will not appreciate you calling me that."

"Just shut up and listen to me. And remember where you are."

"O-okay?" I puzzle.

"There's something we didn't tell you about the night of the...well, you know."

I nod sharply. It's better if no one says it. But my chest constricts in fear at the mention of that night and the grave expression on Kalen's face.

"What?" I ask with trepidation.

"Don't kick off…"

"For god's sake, Kalen! Just tell me already!" I snap.

"Okay, keep your panties on."

"I'm not wearing any."

"What?"

"Kalen, focus!"

"How can I focus when you're dropping bombs like that?!"

"It was a joke, Kalen." I sigh and shake my head at him but a small smile tugs on my lips.

"Well, now I don't know what to believe. I'm going to have to find out for myself." He grins wickedly and slides his hand under my blanket to my thigh. I slap it away with a scowl.

"Okay, fine." It's his turn to sigh now. "But give me a kiss." Before I can ask why he leans over and steals one. "You might not want to kiss me afterwards."

"Kalen—"

"Alright, alright! Man, you sound like my brothers when you say it like that." He takes a deep breath and I see the worry in his eyes. "So, I know you didn't want to talk about that night until Onyx was okay, but when Sawyer and I were coming to find you, we found someone unconscious."

"Okay." I draw out the letters, prompting him to continue.

"It was Baxter."

"Baxter? Was he okay?"

"He barely had a pulse, Amelie."

"What did you do?"

"We argued about it. I wanted to help him. Said you'd kick our asses if anything happened to him."

"That's true… What did Sawyer say?"

"That if Baxter was okay and anything happened to you, he'd kill us for wasting time on him."

"Also true. But I hoped you risked it."

"We pinned our locations on a map, knowing that as soon as help arrived they would track us and find him."

My frown deepens. I'm not happy about it, but I guess I can understand their logic. Plus, if they hadn't arrived when they did, Onyx… No! I shut those thoughts down.

"When help came, Baxter was gone."

"Okay, so he came round and was okay?"

"No one has seen him since, Amelie."

"He always disappears though, doesn't he?"

"Yeah, but he's always contactable. No one has heard from

him."

I shake my head.

"I don't understand what you're saying, Kalen."

"He's missing, Amelie. If it weren't for Sawyer and me confirming we saw him outside of the main building, he would have been presumed dead in the blast by now."

An entirely new kind of rage burns through me. It's white hot and blinding in its intensity.

"Why the hell didn't you tell me!" I whisper-yell, smacking him on the arm. I'm conscious that it's the middle of the night and many passengers are asleep. Typical dick Kalen move, to tell me when I can't flip out.

"Honestly? There was so much going on, and then time had passed and I didn't know how, and...and..."

"Why now?"

"Because we're on a plane and you can't run away or beat the ever living shit out of me."

"When we land, your ass is mine. And I'll be having words with your brothers when I get back to the UK too."

"Sorry."

"You absolute fucking...douche canoe!" I hiss. I'm so mad right now.

I'm mad at Kalen for waiting until I'm trapped in the air to tell me. At the others for not saying anything sooner. At myself for not even thinking of Baxter or trying to reach out to him.

And at Baxter himself.

Because if I know one thing for certain, it's that there's no way in hell Baxter Branson is dead. Which means I'm going to have to give him hell for letting everyone think he is.

When I find him, that is.

Amelie: You know what? You're an asshole. Arsehole. All the fucking holes!

Message undelivered

Amelie: If you're dead, I hope it hurt.

Message undelivered

Amelie: If you're alive, you better be hiding.

Message undelivered

Amelie: Baxter whatever the fuck your middle name is Branson, I'm going to make it my life's mission to hunt you down.

Message undelivered

Amelie: I will peel you alive and wear your skin as a suit.

Message undelivered

Chapter Four

Baxter

"Baxter?" The surprised tone tells me I'm probably the last person he expected to hear from. I have no idea what time it is in the UK. It could be the middle of the night, but I don't give a shit.

"I need…" I hesitate. I almost said a favour, but is my curiosity worth a life? I think probably not. "Information."

There's a pause on the end of the line while I wait for Frost to reply. I can almost feel his reluctance and disapproval coming down the line in waves.

"I see. Can we talk about that in a minute?"

"I don't really—"

"Because we really need to talk about your little disappearing act."

I sigh. Of course he wants to talk about that. I don't give a damn if he traces my location; he's the only person I trust not to reveal it.

"Fine. Off record."

"Of course. I won't be speaking to anyone within The Order.

There's something going on with the board and I'm not sure I trust any of them."

"Trust Amelie. You can trust the Knox boys too – if you have to. Not their grandfather though."

"I wouldn't. He's as bent as a nine bob note. What about the father, Monty?"

"Who says that anymore? I'm undecided about him."

"Okay…so are you having a nice time in the…British Virgin Islands?"

I can't help bite back a smile. You can take the intelligence operative out of the line of duty, but old habits die hard.

"Peachy."

"You're alive then."

"Evidently."

"Why the vanishing act?"

"Long story," I evade. I trust the guy with Amelie's life, but do I trust him with mine? Whoever injected me had an agenda here, but I'm yet to figure out what it is. "So about that information I need…"

"Shoot."

"There's a girl joining me here. I need to know everything about her."

"Okay. Do you have a name?"

"I have two. Raven and Charlotte."

"Two girls?"

"One girl. Two names."

"Odd."

"Right? She's connected to Cordelia cuntface somehow. Allegedly a granddaughter but I'm not convinced."

"Okay. And…erm…is Cuntface her legal surname or…?"

"I forget you don't move in my circles, Frost. You lucky son of a bitch. Try Deighton. Cordelia Cuntface Deighton."

He coughs down a laugh. "Okay, sir. And will this...make us even?"

"We've always been even, Frost. But if you can help me with this and keep watching Amelie for me, I'll owe you one."

"Yes, sir. As soon as she's back, I'll watch over her again."

"Back? What do you mean back? Where the hell is she?" Panic laces my words, making me snap.

"She went away...for a funeral I believe."

"Whose?" There's no way it was one of the Knox brothers; I would have been told. Somehow. Only...I blocked my phone to all Order numbers, didn't I?

"Someone back in her homeland, I believe."

"She went alone?!"

"No. I believe...Kalen accompanied her."

Jesus, it's worse than I thought. What kind of protection is that muppet going to offer?

"I see." My voice is tight with stress. "I'll call you tomorrow, for the information. Don't speak of this conversation to anyone."

I cut the call.

Shit. This isn't good. I'm going to have to speak to Camilla. I bet after everything that happened at the Kessler mansion, she's going to be mighty pissed about this turn of events. And I get to be the lucky guy that gets to fill her in.

Fuck.

Amelie: We buried someone today. I didn't expect to care, but I kept thinking it could so easily have been Onyx. Do you know what happened to him? Do you even care?

Message Undelivered

Amelie: It could have been you. And I'm not okay with that, at all.

Message Undelivered

Amelie: Goddamn it, Batman! I miss you, okay? Just let me know you're alright for fuck's sake!

Message Undelivered

Chapter Five

Amelie

The funeral was nice, as far as funerals go. I mean, I barely even knew the guy. He was definitely part of my brother's crowd. And while I used to try and tag-along with him and Smalls, they definitely had friends I didn't know about. Judging by their reaction, I wouldn't have said this guy was a good friend, but then, why would they ask me to come to the funeral for support if they weren't cut up about his death?

There's so much I don't know about Smalls and Aadi's life. I always knew they sheltered me from a lot. But the crowd gathered today look like some unsavoury characters. Eyes roamed over my body most of the day much to Kalen's disgust. I have to beg him to drop it. I'm even pretty sure I see a few plain clothed cops watching from a distance.

My father's house is packed to the brim with men I don't know, all drinking and telling stories. Chelsea manages to wrangle Kalen into helping her bring out food. I scan the crowd but can't find Smalls anywhere. He's a big dude so he isn't easily missed.

As I head upstairs, the sound of laughter and the beat of some Eminem song fade away. Smalls is sitting on his bed, his hands covering his face. I take a seat beside him, placing my hand on his leg. It's a gesture I've done a million times before, but somehow now it feels wrong. He looks up at me from under his thick lashes, his brown eyes full of sadness. Maybe he is more cut up about this than I originally thought.

"Are you okay?" I ask, and he nods.

"Sometimes this life isn't fair Amelie. It just sucks that his life was cut short. He had a girl at home...and a son." He leans forward and places his forehead against mine. "I'll be okay."

"You know, you really should go shower. You reek of alcohol, pot, and a teenage boy just hitting puberty."

He laughs at my comment. "I'm glad you came back," he says, standing.

"I'm happy too, even if it is under shitty circumstances. Kalen did have to drag me here though."

"He doesn't seem so bad – typical rich boy – but not bad. I'm glad you're happy. But watch out for Aadi. He hasn't forgotten about Christmas morning, and he may be planning a surprise for your boy."

"I could tell by the look in his eyes. He thinks he's sneaky, but he can't fool me."

Smalls laughs. He has always tried to be Switzerland between our pranks.

"Can I ask you something?" Smalls asks hesitantly.

"Sure. Shoot." I try to keep my tone neutral but a little dread creeps in. I hope he's not going to question my relationship with the guys.

"Are you coming back? Here, I mean. When you graduate?"

"I—"

"I thought so. It's okay you know. I could tell. You were just so damn eager to get on that plane when that teacher dude showed up. You practically ran for the door."

"It wasn't like that. At all."

"Amelie, you're a runner. Shit got real with your dad, and instead of sorting it out like an adult, you ran like a baby."

"First, babies can't run."

"You sound like that asshole downstairs."

"And second, it wasn't like that at all. They told me that the teacher died. He *died*, Smalls. And while I logically know that you can't die from eating a few dozen cookies with Weed in them, I...I wanted to save you."

"The dude was diabetic or had some underlying medical condition. That's why he died."

"It doesn't matter. I thought you were going to prison if I told the truth, and I couldn't handle that." I pause and consider his words. Then I confess, "I ran when Onyx was hurt too. Not when I found him. But when help came and they said he might not make it, I—"

"Sssh, it's okay. I can understand that with everything that's happened to you. He will too. But are you telling me that the only reason you went back was because you were trying to save me?"

I shrug. I mean, I'm glad I did. But it's not the *only* reason.

"You know I'd do it a hundred times over for you and Aadi. But I also have unfinished business."

"With them?"

"With Laura."

"Amelie—"

"No. She has to pay for what she's done."

Smalls sighs but nods his head in acceptance.

"Now can I ask you a question?"

"Shoot."

"What's with all the dodgy types at the funeral?"

"I don't know, I can't control who comes to the guy's send off can I?" He looks away and I can tell he's lying, the question is why. I decide to let it go for now.

"Will you wait for me to shower?" He asks, changing the topic and lumbering to his feet. I nod and he walks away.

While he's gone, I look around his room. Not much has changed since we moved here. There's fewer posters of half-naked women on his walls and a bigger bed now, but that's all.

I pick up the photo on his bedside table and smile. I remember the day this was taken. It wasn't long before my attack. I look happy in the picture, clinging to his back like a baby monkey. I'm not sure I've smiled like that in a long time.

Smalls' phone vibrates and I glance at the screen. It's Yasmin, a friend of his. He mentioned she couldn't make it today.

"Hey," I say, deciding to answer the call.

"Amelie?" she asks cautiously.

"Yep, it's me."

"Oh my god, it's been so long. Smalls has told me all about your UK adventure and those boys."

I laugh. Of course he has. "It has been an interesting adjustment."

"How is he? I feel like a shit friend for not being able to come, but so much is going on here."

"He'll be fine, I think it's more the shock that the guy wasn't much older than him and had a family."

Smalls walks back into the room, a towel wrapped around his

waist and I blink. We may have drawn a line and know where each of us stands but I'm not immune to all that.

"Uh, Smalls just got out of the shower so I'll pass you over. It was nice talking to you again."

"You too," she says and I hand the phone to Smalls, who looks down at the caller ID and smiles.

"Hey shorty, what's up?" That's what I love about him; no matter how he feels, his tone doesn't give away his pain. Always trying to protect other people.

"I'll come back up and check on you soon," I whisper and he nods. I close his door to give him privacy.

I don't know much about his and Yasmin's friendship. All I know is that her dad helped Smalls a lot before he came to live with Chelsea. Saved his ass a few times too. I've got respect for the entire family for that. Lord knows, Smalls needs some good people in his life. Especially now.

I slip into my room to make a phone call. First, I try Baxter's number but it's disconnected. Wanker. So I call Sawyer. I'm not ready to face the twins.

"Hey, how much do you need?"

"Huh?" I ask, Sawyer's opening line throwing me for a loop.

"Well, you've been there twenty-four-hours now, and you're calling, so I'm assuming it's because you need bail money for Kalen."

I laugh.

"Close. He won't get arrested, he'll get a casket." I stop laughing. Jesus, that was in poor taste.

"Don't worry about it," Sawyer says gently, reading my mind as always. "What do you need?"

"Information."

"Okay, shoot."

"I need to know where Baxter is. I have to speak to him."

"I wish we knew—"

"Speak to Jasper and Frost. Someone knows something. I have to speak to him. It's urgent."

"Okay, leave it with me. I'll text you a number when I get one."

"Thanks."

"No problem, Amelie. Have a great time."

"Is…everyone okay?" I hesitate, not wanting to seem only interested in Onyx, but of course, Sawyer sees through that too.

"Onyx is fine, Amelie. All of us are. Even Marshmallow."

"I miss him, give him a kiss from me."

"You better mean the damn dog, I'm not snogging any of my brothers for you!" We laugh and it feels good.

"I have to go."

"No worries. Miss you."

"You too."

With a smile on my face, I cut the call and head out of my room and down the corridor to go back downstairs, but stop short when I spy a familiar figure coming towards me. Familiar and unwelcome.

"What the hell are you doing here?" I hiss at Sarah, Smalls' ex. Or Skanky Sarah as I like to call her.

"Do you mind? Show some respect, we just buried one of our own today."

"Yeah, from what I heard he had a girl and a son at home. That's a new level of low, isn't it? Aspiring to be a homewrecker."

Sarah's eyes flash with anger but I don't give a fuck. I want to provoke her. I disliked her from the moment I laid eyes on her and now I'm allowed to. I hope she starts something; I have new skills I can showcase.

"It's none of your damn business what was going on between Brenton and me!"

"No, but when you started screwing around behind Smalls' back, *that* became my damn business. I'd like to say I'm going to get payback because you hurt him, but in all honesty, he didn't give that much of a fuck about you. So now this is just going to be for fun." Channelling my inner Branson, I give slutface Sarah my best psychopath smile, revelling in the nervous way she swallows.

This is going to be fun.

Amelie: Am I a bad person for starting a fight at a funeral?

Message undelivered

Amelie: I mean, the bitch totally had it coming. And I only made her bleed a little before I was pulled off her.

Message undelivered

Amelie: I gave her a psychopath smile. You know, The Baxter Branson Special? It got me rethinking the offer I declined earlier… burning the world to the ground with you could be fun.

Message undelivered

Chapter Six

Baxter

"Mr Branson, sir?" A formal but scared sort of voice interrupts my internet stalking. I'm reading through the intel Frost sent me on this Raven/Charlotte chick. It's fascinatingly vague, which in itself piques my interest.

"What?" I snap, hating the distraction.

"You have a phone call, sir. Sorry, sir." The terrified receptionist? Maid? – Fuck, I don't know who she is, but I do remember sleeping with her a time or two – holds the phone out to me in trembling hands. I sneer at her and snatch the mobile up. Fucking pathetic.

"You didn't really think you could hide from me?" A voice interrupts before I can say anything.

I stay silent.

"You can't almost die on me and not tell me."

Amelie.

Jesus, even on the other side of the world I can't get away from her.

"I didn't think you would care," I say dismissively. And it's true. Why would she?

"Are you fucking serious?!" she yells, sounding way angrier than I expected. It makes me smile. She's always so hot-headed. The Order will hate that.

"You're one of them now," I reply, knowing that it'll rile her up even more, just wanting to see her reaction. She'll never be one of them, not really. She could be the best thing to ever happen to The Order. Which I would love to see, just from a distance. Regardless of who's in charge or the changes they make, I can't go back. Can't get sucked in again. Not even for her.

"Again, are you fucking serious?! I'm still me, and the last time I checked *you* still had the same tattoo as them."

Touché. I don't say anything though. I'm too stubborn for that.

"Where are you?" she asks softly. I sigh. "In all seriousness, are you okay?"

"This line isn't secure. We'll talk when we're back in school."

"You're coming back then? I was worried you wouldn't."

"For now I will. But I'm not making any promises to stay."

"Thank you." Her reply is so soft I have to strain to hear it but when I do, it does something strange to my chest.

"I have to go, but I'll see you soon enough. Oh, and Amelie?"

"Yeah?"

"Thank you for giving a damn."

I hang up so she doesn't have to reply and hand the phone back to the member of staff. A grin stretches across my face and I feel better than I have in weeks. Lighter somehow.

I decide I'll go for a swim. It's time to stop sulking about my attack and to start building my strength back up to what it was so that when I find the motherfuckers responsible, I'm able to actually make good on my threat to fuck them up.

On my way to the pool I bump into Cordelia who does a double take when she sees me.

"Has hell frozen over?" she asks in a cold, scathing tone she reserves for when my grandfather isn't around. I wonder if he has the measure of her, really, or if he'd be shocked to see this side of her. I consider this to be her real face, rather than the one she shows my grandfather, but they've been together so long, maybe she doesn't even know anymore.

"You're still breathing so it can't have," I reply curtly.

"But you're smiling." Her face is a picture.

"Of course I'm smiling," I reply smoothly. "Your granddaughter arrives today and I can't wait to *meet* her." I lick my lips, and the old woman shudders from head to toe. She doesn't engage me though, which is surprising, so I push past her and head to the nearest pool, which just so happens to be my favourite.

My favourite pool is down by some of the beach huts but rarely used. It's secluded, surrounded on all sides by thick vegetation. It feels like my own slice of paradise, especially when I enter the clearing and see the still water glistening in the sunlight. It looks cool and inviting, just what I need.

Stripping my clothes off quickly, I chuck them carelessly onto a sun lounger and stand at the water's edge. My toes curl over the edge, and I take a moment to breathe deeply before launching myself into the pool in a sleek dive.

The water is a refreshing wake up call. I need to get my head out of my ass. Grandfather is right, I have been sulking, but that ends now. Since when has Baxter Branson ever been a victim? Never. So I'm not about to start now. Smoothly swimming laps,

I take time to clear my head and come up with a plan of action.

Of course what I told Amelie is true. I will go back to Knox. I'll finish my sentence, get my degree and graduate. Hopefully, if I tell Grandfather I want to concentrate on his businesses for a few years, he'll let The Order stuff go, for a while at least. Plus, being close to Order HQ will put me in the best position possible to find how deep the corruption runs. I need answers. Not only about the blast, but about who targeted me and why. Can't do that from a sun lounger sipping an Old Fashioned.

And then there's Amelie. I guess she's going to need someone to look out for her still. I wasn't lying when I told Frost to trust the Knox brothers – I do trust them where she's concerned – but do I trust them to take over the running of The Order with Amelie at the helm? I'm not sure.

They profess to love her, but they have fucked her over before. And is love enough? I'd easily argue it isn't. Not if their daddy dearest wants to pull the strings. Let's face it, his 'sons' have always been his puppets, so why would that suddenly change? I'm fairly sure Monty wanted to pull Amelie's strings, but once he found she wasn't so easy to control, he used his sons to do his dirty work. Sure, they might have real feelings for her, and may even love her, but would they choose Amelie over their dear father to whom they owe everything?

I think not.

So it's decided then. I'll go back after Easter Break, finish the school year, keep an eye on Amelie and the Knox family, find out what's going on with The Order, and hopefully find out why someone tried to kill me. Easy.

I actually feel surprisingly better after I'm done with my swim. I think the planning helped, but I definitely need some time in the gym. That can wait til tomorrow. I won't be any use to anyone if I start by overdoing it. I'll grab some lunch back at my beachside pad, and then I'll scope out the new chick and see what she's like.

There was a disturbing lack of photos in the information Frost sent me, so I'm not sure what to expect. I'm guessing a little miniature version of cuntface Cordelia, with an equally large stick up her ass. I snort at the image. Be fun to fuck her with it though.

Amelie: Hey, you never did say where you are…

Message undelivered

Amelie: Seriously?! You're still ignoring my messages? Even though we spoke on the phone. Unblock me you wanker!

Message undelivered

Amelie: You know what? I think I actually prefer our friendship like this… you know, you not talking. Especially 'cause you were such a dick the last time we did speak at the party. Asshole

Message undelivered

Chapter Seven

Amelie

"I can't believe you pulled me off her." I throw my fiercest glare at Aadi.

"Yeah. Seriously not cool, bro," Kalen chimes in. He doesn't seem as angry about it as I am. "Girl on girl fighting is hot."

"Dick." I throw my bag of frozen peas at him.

"Monster cock, get it right." Kalen winks.

"Ugh, will you both shut up!" Aadi snaps. "I can't believe you started a fight at a funeral."

"Technically it was at the wake—"

"And she certainly put the 'fun' back in funeral," Kalen quips. Aadi glares at him but Smalls snorts.

"Oh, I suppose you think this is funny, do you, big guy?" Aadi snaps, rounding on Smalls. "Two chicks fighting over you?"

"Technically, there were four of us."

"What?"

"Well, I caught Slaggy Sarah sneaking around upstairs – probably looking to hook back up with Smalls since Brenton is off the cards – but what I didn't know was that Crystal had seen her downstairs and followed her too."

"Okay. That I can understand. Crystal's a psycho. She's always down to maim someone. But you said four."

"Well, that's where it gets interesting. Another girl also saw and followed. Some chick named Katie. She doesn't like Sarah either, which makes her good in my books."

"So all three of you jumped her?"

"No…that implies there was a surprise attack. I confronted slutface Sarah and told her she had it coming. I was pretty up front about it." I shrug because I truly feel no shame about the whole thing. My only regret was that Aadi broke the whole thing up before I could do any real damage. I got a few good hits in though, busted her nose, and I'm pretty sure Crystal stabbed her a little bit. Katie was a bit savage with the hair pulling but hey, whatever floats her boat.

Aadi kicked Sarah out straight after. Didn't even give her a tissue to stem the bleeding. He may be giving me hell now, but he showed total solidarity to me in front of the fuckface.

Smalls and Kalen are pissing themselves now, high fiving and passing out more beers.

"Lighten up, bro. It was a fun show."

"Stop calling me that! I'm not your damn brother!" Aadi's temple vein is large and throbbing; a sure sign he's going to seriously lose his shit.

"Well, technically you kind of are. Or will be. Our parents are going to marry. And if they don't, I'm going to marry Amelie. I'll marry her anyway, even if she's my sister. Incest is best, right! So you're kinda stuck with me."

"Does he ever shut up?" Aadi groans.

"No. Just roll with it and life'll be easier," I promise.

"I hate you all." Kalen pouts.

"Hey!"

"Except Smalls. He's cool. Even if he has a tiny dick."

"Erm, what?" I blink in shock at Kalen. He is so barking up the wrong tree there. Although...I guess next to his, even above average might seem small.

"You must have, right? Why else would they call you Smalls?" Kalen asks, turning to raise a brow at him.

"Have you seen the size of me?" Small returns with a smirk.

"Erm...yeah..."

"So it's ironic you moron." He snorts.

"If you say so," Kalen replies in a tone which clearly says he doesn't believe him. "Show me your dick to prove otherwise."

"I'm not showing you my dick! I barely know you."

"But you would if we were better acquainted?" Kalen grins.

"Babygirl! Make him stop talking," Smalls begs me.

"Oh, no." I laugh. "You got yourself into this one big guy, you can get yourself out of it."

"Well, at least tell him my cock isn't small!"

"How the hell would Milly know what your cock is like, Smalls?" My brother growls, instantly getting riled up.

We freeze like kangaroos caught in headlights, eyes locked on one another. Aadi might know about our repressed feelings for one another after the Christmas Day debacle, but he doesn't know about that one time we slept together after my attack.

"Don't be a moron. We lived together and you guys are gross. I've seen you both naked more times than I'd care to count!" I laugh nervously. "You need to use a towel when you shower."

Aadi glowers at us like he isn't buying it, but lets it slide, much to my relief. Thankfully, Kalen's annoying tendency to over talk kicks back in and distracts us all. Thank god he didn't spill my secrets.

"So now that the sad shit is over and done with, our holiday can start properly! I want to do all the proper Australian stuff, live like a real local. I want to eat Vegemite for breakfast, lunch and tea. I want to pet all the dangerous animals. I want to ride kangaroos, see the desert, go surfing, cook shrimp on a barbie, drink Fosters, and get a tan…Where do we start?!"

Aadi, Smalls and I all stare at Kalen in astonishment.

"Wow, Kalen. Did you google Australian stereotypes or something?" I ask.

"Or just how to be a racist ass?" Smalls joins in.

"Milly, where the fuck did you find this cunt?" Aadi asks, shaking his head.

"Dude!" Kalen gasps, looming affronted. "That's a bit harsh."

"Cunt means something different here, Kalen. We sprinkle that shit around like confetti. It's practically a term of endearment."

"So if I call you my sweet little cunt—"

"Try calling my sister that and let's see how many teeth you still have," Aadi yells, jumping to his feet, his chair scraping noisily across the floor.

"Okay!" I jump in, trying to keep the peace. "I'm calling time out. Kalen, we actually have a birthday party to arrange. Chelsea's niece is six tomorrow and we're holding the party here this weekend. You can help me get things ready today."

"A kid's party?" He wrinkles his nose up in distaste. "That wasn't exactly what I had in mind for living it up down under!"

"Well, you wanted the authentic Australian experience so you're going to get it. Family means everything here, so get on board with that and shut the fuck up."

"Aye aye, Captain." He salutes me, sarcastic little shit.

"Be good, or I won't let you have any Fairy Bread."

Amelie: Dick. Expect random insults until I hear from you.

Message delivered

Amelie: Wanker.

Message delivered

Amelie: Tosspot.

Message delivered

Amelie: Cocksucker.

Message delivered

Baxter: Seriously? Is that the best you've got? Thought Kalen would have rubbed off on you a little more than that by now...

Message delivered

Amelie: You titwanking arsebadgering knob jockey of a cunting cum stain!

Message delivered

Amelie: Holy shit! You replied! You're getting my messages!

Message delivered

Baxter: No shit, Sherlock. That's why I'm Batman and you're Robin.

Message delivered

Amelie: I'm so glad you're alive. But I'M Batman. And I'm going to kill you.

Message delivered

Chapter Eight

Baxter

I've been summoned to dinner. Actually, my grandfather summoned me to a family dinner, but as his whore is going to be there, I refuse to acknowledge a familial connection. I've been ordered to dress up, which is utterly ridiculous. I always look smart. I take pride in my impeccable appearance. I can, however, understand the mandate to be on my best behaviour. I'm just not going to abide by it.

I think tonight is finally the night I get to officially meet the whore's granddaughter. I say officially, because she's been on this goddamn island a week already and while they've done their best to keep her away from me, I've been able to snag glimpses of her here and there.

Colour me intrigued. I want to know why she's here. I think she's hiding or on the run or something, but even my Order connections couldn't turn up any dirt on her. Which in itself is suspicious.

Besides, this whole thing is an absolute joke. First, I get told to stay away from the girl, and then I'm summoned to have dinner with her.

As if that wasn't bad enough, when I get to the main house, Grandfather ushers me into the informal dining room and I discover it's set for two. Then he leaves me, to go and greet his guests.

What the hell is he playing at? He obviously has some sort of agenda here. Why else would he have had a complete 180? I pray The Order isn't involved somehow. I can't fuck with the girl if she's somehow tied to The Order. I'm pretty sure my life is dangling by a thread with them anyway, and if they're going to such great pains to hide this girl's identity...well, I'm just saying, no pussy is worth all that.

When I hear voices in the hallway outside, I sneak over to peek through the small crack where Grandfather didn't quite shut the door. I smirk as the object of my interest recognises my grandfather and her jaw goes slack. Her bright green eyes are like saucers. Interesting. So she's never met him before but she recognises him. That's good; she'll be easier to seduce if she knows who I am and what I'm heir to. Chicks dig that rich heir shit.

I have to move away from the door when I see how Cordelia and my grandfather are looking at one another. It's enough to put anyone off their dinner, and I'm actually quite looking forward to this.

The girl looks beautiful. That's my first thought when the doors swing open and they step across the threshold. She looks surprised to see me, obviously unaware of my presence – which is good because it means she hasn't noticed my...observing her all week. I definitely wouldn't call it stalking. More, keeping tabs on. A friendly watchful eye.

Finally, seeing her up close and from the front, it's like all the little missing pieces of a puzzle come together and I get the overall picture. Before I just had snapshots, flashes, glimpses, but now I can stare to my heart's content. She's stunning. But not what I was expecting.

Her cheekbones are high, her nose straight. She has the perfect blow job pout that could keep a man hard for days. Her long black hair flashes with shades of blue even in the intimate lighting of the dining room. I can just imagine wrapping those long tresses around my fist to control her every movement. My dormant dick starts to stir like a predator coming out of hibernation.

I knew she had shapely legs from watching her sunbathe by the pool, but now in her short but elegant – and clearly grandmother approved – dress, I can't take my eyes off them. In heels, she's a vision. I hope she keeps them on later while we're fucking. I may have to insist on it.

"Ah, Charlotte. Sorry, Raven." My grandfather getting flustered pulls me out of my fantasies. Shame. "This is my grandson, Baxter. Baxter, this is Cordelia's granddaughter, Raven."

I watch her closely as she cringes at the way my grandfather muddles her name up. I feel her eyeing me wearily. She doesn't like his slip up, she knows I'll have questions and she doesn't want to open up to me. I can see how guarded she is in everything from her shuttered eyes to the tense way she's holding herself.

I stand to greet her, always polite and on ceremony when my grandfather is around. It's one of many roles I'm used to playing. So many roles. In The Order, I'm the silent assassin, ruthless and efficient. To the Knox brothers, I'm a misconceived threat to the girl they love. To Amelie I'm...a friend. That's not a role I'm used to playing, but I'm finding it quite enjoyable.

The girl is staring at me, for a beat too long too. I don't see the usual appreciation flare in her eyes. Nor is there the cold calculation of a gold digger. She doesn't even look afraid of me, like the people who know what I'm capable of always do.

No. There's simply a hard, wary defiance in her eyes that piques my interest. I want to get inside this girl's head, not just her pants. I could crack open her skull and watch her secrets spill alongside her blood. She would make a pretty addition to—

I shut those dark thoughts down. I don't do that anymore. Well, I don't do it often. The Order gave me a legitimate outlet for those urges, and I haven't lost control since I painted Amelie's mural with Knox blood. And no one even died that time so maybe I'm getting better. It would be both a dream come true and a crying shame if I was.

Although, I haven't got my hands on whoever drugged me yet. They're in for a whole new world of unimaginable pain.

The girl in front of me intrigues me. I want to know her secrets, not spill her blood. I repeat that to myself a couple of times over until I almost believe it.

I gaze at her with a cold, fierce intensity, devoid of all expression, until I know I've got my darkness back under control. It doesn't help that she shivers and my cock twitches, like a bear stretching when it first wakes up or some shit.

"Nice to meet you," I say smoothly, slipping into full charm mode. I even put some expression into my tone. If my grandfather wants to switch plans from keeping her hidden from me, to thrusting her into my path, I'll play along and he can reap the consequences.

I hold out my hand for her to shake, not moving out from behind the table to keep my curious dick hidden. She doesn't move for a beat, then shakes her head and steps forward quickly to place her hand in mine. Her silken skin burns mine like fire, and I can't help but squeeze her small delicate bones in a crushing handshake. I like the feel of her under my hands. I want more.

"And you?"

I bite back a knowing smirk when her reply comes out as a question. So she's not completely immune to me either then.

Feeling our grandparents disapproving eyes upon us, I raise the back of her hand to my lips and kiss it, all while holding her gaze. It's a chivalrous, dead move, not really me at all, but I love how uncomfortable it makes everyone in the room.

Keeping hold of her hand, I use it to pull her towards me. Even in her heels she had to go up onto tiptoes to reach as I draw her closer and closer. She's bent over the table and I finally get a good look down her top. I'm not disappointed. Beneath the modest neckline she has an excellent rack. What I wouldn't give to be standing behind her ass right now though. The only thing I'd love more than to fuck her from behind over this table, would be to lay her out on it and make *her* my twelve-course-meal.

She freaks and tries to pull away as I lean in to kiss her, but I still have hold of her hand. She can't do anything without making a scene, and I'm *just* trying to be polite. As I close the distance between us, the panic in her eyes and her air of desperation teases and provokes me even more. Fuck decorum. I deliberately aim for her lips.

And they're so fucking soft and pillowy I know I'll die if I don't get to experience them wrapped around the base of my cock.

I'm so distracted by that thought, my grip loosens on hers. Unfortunately, she chooses that exact moment to yank her hand from mine and she sends a wine glass clattering across the table. I grin.

"Ah, young love," my grandfather titters with a smirk. I cock my head and study him, curious. The girl sends him a death glare. He ignores us both and turns to Cordelia. "Shall we dine in the formal room and leave these two to get to know each other a little better?"

She desperately makes eyes at her grandmother, probably begging them to stay and not leave her alone with me, but Cordelia only has eyes for my grandfather, and my grandfather has a plan. I'm on his side with this one. Go. Leave. Thank you for bringing me a nice little lamb to play with.

The door closes and the girl in front of me swallows nervously. A wicked grin stretches across my face. I'm going to have some fun tonight.

Amelie: You'll help me get away with it, if I kill someone, right? Even in international waters?

Message delivered

Baxter: Who?

Message delivered

Amelie: Kalen. He's driving me crazy. Who thought he'd be the best choice of travelling companion for me?

Message delivered

Baxter: I wondered the same thing myself. If you kill him, I've got your back. But I'd rather you let me join in on the fun

Message delivered

Chapter Nine

Amelie

It takes us a couple of days to prepare the party for Kelsie, Chelsea's niece. We have to run errands all over town, and Kalen is by my side every step of the way. And he's an incredible pain in the ass the entire time, whining and moaning all day long.

"I want Fairy Bread! You promised!"

"Why can't we get the blue piñata?"

"I want the big bouncy castle!"

He thinks he can just pout and flounce to get his own way, and when that doesn't work, he throws money at everything. Seriously, the boy needs to be put on an allowance. A small one. He's spent more on this party for some kid he doesn't know, than my family has to feed everyone in an entire month.

I know he means well, but it is exhausting. I do give in and let him hire whatever the hell he wants from the jumping castle people – stipulating that it needs to fit in the garden and there still be room for the adults and the BBQ.

Chelsea, on the other hand, adores him. They go to Coles to get the party food and their butcher to get the meat, which I know she would never usually do. She always used to say why spend the extra money when it's the way you cook it that creates the flavour. Maybe she's trying to impress Kalen. It backfired on her when he fills two entire trollies with items – one with all kinds of crap for the kids and the other full of meat and seafood for the adults to barbecue – before picking up the bill.

"Oh my, I don't know where I'm going to store all of this," Chelsea says as we enter the kitchen with the final bags from the car. The bottles of booze clink loudly as I put them down. I snapped at Kalen earlier, telling him to quit wasting money on crap for kids. If he wants to part with his not-so-hard-earned cash, he could spend it on booze for the adults. Once he realised there would be alcohol at a kid's party, he got even more carried away. Hence why Chelsea's kitchen now looks like a farmer's market crossed with a brewery.

"Yeah, sorry, I can't help you there." Kalen laughs. "But I'll sure as hell help eat and drink it all tomorrow. Can I man the barbie?"

"No!" I yell at the same time Chelsea says, "sure." I glare at her and shake my head. That is not a good idea. My dad will be pissed; manning the barbecue is his pride and joy. Chelsea knows that, so she must really be trying to make Kalen feel welcome to give up my dad's favourite job to him.

"Maybe Kalen could be in charge of the kid's table instead," I offer, trying to keep the peace. I'm pretty sure if we put Kalen in charge of the barbecue everyone will go home with food poisoning. We never had a BBQ at Monty's house but I noticed one in the garden. It used charcoal. That's almost a dirty word here, unless you're camping and literally have no other options.

❤ ❤ ❤

"What the hell is that?" Kalen hisses at me when my dad heads inside to get a beer.

"What?"

"That!" He points to the metal monstrosity that we use for feeding our extended family.

"It's the barbecue." I look at him like he's stupid.

"That is not a barbecue." He frowns, shakes his head, sneers. "Where's the charcoal?"

"We use gas," I tell him simply, shrugging my shoulders.

"Wow. I feel betrayed." He places his hand over his heart. "Like, by your entire nation."

"Huh?"

"You're supposed to be these famous barbecuers and you're imposters...it's not a barbecue at all. It's a grill! A hob! An outdoor cooker! That's the ultimate betrayal."

"You're crazy." I shake my head at his theatrics. "It's just the way it's done here. And don't let my dad hear you dissing his barbecue. I swear he loves that thing more than Aadi and me."

Kalen's still staring at the barbecue like it's going to bite him so I know I made the right call to put him on the kid's food instead. Not that my dad would ever have let him cook.

"It's almost time, the guests should be arriving any minute," I tell Kalen.

"Is it ok? Does it look ok? Do we have enough food? Should I have hired jugglers to entertain?" I can't help but laugh over the way Kalen is stressing about 'his' party. He's committed to ensuring all the kids have a great time. It's pretty darn adorable actually.

"Relax. Everything's perfect. Now...did you want to try the Fairy Bread before the kids get here and demolish it all?"

His eyes light up at the bribe I've been holding over his head for days now, so I cave and finally let him try a slice. I mean, it's just bread and butter covered in rainbow coloured sprinkles, but I knew he'd love it.

He does. He practically *inhales* half the loaf of bread before I can swipe the plate away from him.

"Oh my god," he groans orgasmically.

"Kalen! Save some for the children."

"Give it back! It's mine. They can get their own fairy heaven bread."

"It's just called Fairy Bread you idiot."

"Nope. It's heaven. I love how it crunches when I chew."

"Well, I do not!" I laugh. "Close your mouth while you chew."

"It's sooooo good, Amelie." He closes his eyes in bliss. "You should have some."

"Thanks, I'll pass. I grew out of eating that when I was eight."

"You don't know what you're missing." Suddenly his eyes open and he's staring at me with a wild, wired kind of look.

"I need to make more fairy food!"

"What? No, Kalen, you don't."

"Fairy juice! I want to make fairy juice. I can mix soda and sprinkles!" He races into the house excitedly, calling out for Chelsea. I shake my head, letting him go. He can be her annoying problem for a while.

An hour later, I watch with barely concealed amusement as Kalen screams and charges at the jumping castle, twenty sugar-hyped kids following in his wake. They're enamoured by him, staring at him like he's a god or something.

I sip my Corona and lime and let him get on with it. If he wants to provide free party entertainment, there isn't an adult here who will stop him. I glance around the back yard and see everyone is having way more fun at this party than we usually do for the kids' events. Kalen and Chelsea went all out on the food, the decorations, the gifts...everything.

I'm groaning under the weight of the platter of seafood I just polished off when Aadi and Smalls come sit by me.

"What the fuck is wrong with that guy, Milly?" My brother asks, shaking his head. I laugh.

"He's just having fun, letting off some steam."

"Is he always like this?" Smalls joins in.

"Pretty much, only he doesn't have such a captive audience at home. His brothers tend to get tired of his crap much sooner and shut him down."

"Home?" Aadi says sharply, making me cringe.

"You know what I mean. We were talking about Kalen, the UK is his home."

"So long as you remember that *this* is your home."

I nod to keep him happy, but I'm not convinced. Knox is my home for the next three years. Maybe longer. And what about The Order? What then? Do I have to stay in the UK because I'm part of that now? They say home is where the heart is...if that's true, the UK is fast becoming my home.

"I'm surprised anyone can shut him down," Smalls says. "He seems out of control to me."

"He has ADHD," I explain.

"Milly! Do you have any idea how much sugar he's had?!"

I shrug. "Relax. It's a party and he's on holiday."

"He knows how to throw a kid's party though, I'll give him

that." Smalls smirks, but I can tell he's impressed that Chelsea and her niece have had such a lovely time. "I just thought, with how all out he's gone, that he would have hired a clown too."

I laugh.

"He's terrified of clowns. Some stupid shit when he was younger. He made me promise we wouldn't have any at this party."

"You don't say…" Aadi grins wickedly and I know he's plotting some prank for Kalen. I could intervene and save him, but he said he wanted the authentic Aussie experience, and getting pranked by Aadi is very much a part of that.

"He's going to be bouncing off the walls all night," Smalls points out.

"He can't do any harm," I reply.

"No. But I might kill him," Aadi growls, glancing at the jumping castle where Kalen has taught the kids some annoying song and they're all belting it out at the top of their lungs.

Thankfully, once the guests all leave, Kalen does deflate a little. He definitely likes having an audience to perform to. I watch as he carries a load of empty bottles to the bin and on his way back, grabs an armful of plates to take inside. Chelsea stops him, takes them from him and kisses him on the cheek. He turns to face me, a massive beaming grin on his face.

"I think she likes me!"

"She does. But Chelsea likes everyone." His face falls like I just kicked his puppy and I sigh. "But the kiss? That means you're family now. Not everyone gets that." He perks back up before grabbing my hand and pulling me to my feet.

"Come on!"

"Where?"

"On the bouncy castle, of course!"

"Kalen, we don't call it that. And it's for kids. We have to let it down before the guy comes to collect it."

"Nah, I rented it for twenty-four-hours. I wasn't sure what time the party would finish so I just said pick it up in the morning."

I shake my head at him, because of course he did, and let him pull me over to the giant purple monstrosity filling the garden. I quickly slip off my shoes and follow him into the enclosed space.

"I haven't been on one of these since I was little," I tell him.

"You're still little." He snorts. Dick.

"Kalen! What the hell are you doing?" He's started to remove his pants. Holy crap, why is he getting naked in my garden? How much sugar did he have? Has he been drinking too? My panic lessens somewhat when he stops after just removing his pants, but he's commando so I get distracted by his cock. It really is mighty fine, even at half-mast. He laughs, chucks his pants through the small opening onto the jumping castle, grabs my hands and starts to jump.

"This is so much fun!" He laughs.

"It is, but why are you half naked?"

Before he can answer there's an urgent cry "Milly!" and Aadi's head appears through the mesh door.

"What the fuck are you doing with your pants off and my sister in here?" He yells at Kalen, climbing in so that Smalls can follow. I giggle at the way Smalls has to twist and turn to squeeze his broad shoulders through the small gap.

"Well this is cosy."

"Shut up, Milly. You're in trouble here too."

"Me? What have I done?"

"You're having sex on a jumping castle."

"Erm, Aadi, I love you brother. But if this is how you have sex, I think you've been doing it wrong."

Smalls and Kalen laugh, Aadi glowers at me.

"Dude, relax. I'm not having my wicked way with your sister. It's just a pants off, dance off."

"What?"

"You know… jam out with your ham out? Funk out with your junk out? Rock out with your cock—"

"Yeah! I get it!" Aadi snaps. "What I don't get is *why?*"

"Amelie, does anyone not willing to helicopter their dick around to cheer you up, even really care about you?" Kalen grins at me. Tears are streaming down my face, he cracks me up so much.

Smalls is eyeing Kalen's cock with a fascinated kind of horror.

"I take it back, you win. I'm not small but that thing is a beast."

"Monster, dude, it's a monster. Come bounce with us."

"Not til you put that weapon away, someone could get skewered on it."

"Maybe later." Kalen winks at me.

"You will not touch my sister!" Aadi screams, charging at Kalen. He dives, wrapping his arms around Kalen's waist and tackling him to the ground. Brave move, I can't help but think as my brother gets a face full of monster cock.

Even though Kalen's dick is out, the pair of them start wrestling. It's ridiculously immature, but my side soon hurts from laughing. Kalen keeps insisting Aadi doesn't hit his face, screaming like a girl. Smalls just has this bemused 'what the fuck?!' look on his face.

Eventually they tire but not before Aadi punches him in the

gut and says to keep his hands off his sister.

"She's my sister too, *brother*," Kalen gasps.

Which earns him a second punch.

Amelie: I'm seriously having second thoughts about this...

Message delivered

Baxter: Too late now... Blood in, blood out, right?

Message delivered

Amelie: I meant coming to Australia with Kalen, you dick!

Message delivered

Baxter: Seriously? That should be the least of your worries. Got any gang insignia tattooed on yourself lately?

Message delivered

Amelie: If we're going to be friends you have got to get over your issues.

Message delivered

Baxter: What issues?!

Message delivered

Amelie: Where do I even start?! By the way, what is your middle name?

Message delivered

Baxter: *message undelivered*

Message delivered

Amelie: Ha-ha. I'll find out one way or another. How did you get it wiped from your file?

Message delivered

Baxter: Do friends always ask this many questions? Because I'm seriously having second thoughts about this.

Message delivered

Amelie: Ha fucking Ha. You know, you can go off some people...

Message delivered

Baxter: Please fucking do.

Message delivered

Chapter Ten

Baxter

With impeccable timing like always, as soon as we are seated, the doors at the far end of the room fly open and the servers enter with the first course. I nod my head in silent thanks as the first plate is placed before me, then I sit and wait. Even once the staff are gone, I wait. I watch. She grows more and more uncomfortable.

Finally, she begins the starter. I think it's so that she doesn't have to look at me any longer. I wish I could eat, but my brain is too busy taking in every inch of her. I just sit and stare at her, elbows on the table, fingertips together, resting against my chin. I'm plotting.

"What's up with the name thing?" I ask. We've been silent for minutes and I'm just not comfortable making small talk. It's not something I often have to do. Usually people are either too scared to talk to me, or too in awe. Those who are brave enough, I quickly shut down. So having to initiate conversation at an intimate dinner for two? Pure hell. I'd rather have a sleepover with Kalen Knox than have to do this.

"What's up with the name Baxter?" she bites back. Okay, she *really* doesn't want to talk about it. "Your parents really like soup or something?"

I chuckle lightly, unable to help myself. She's the first person to ever connect my name to the Scottish soup company, usually people are too obsessed with the Branson name to consider much else. It's a coincidence though, my mother just really liked the alliteration.

"Touché," I say, still laughing slightly. "So you don't want to talk about that then. What shall we talk about?" She shrugs and keeps eating.

"You a vampire or something?" she asks me. I snort back a derisive laugh. Is she for real right now? Doesn't she know people are monstrous enough without inventing new creatures to terrify people?

"Pardon?"

"The not eating thingy." She waves her fork around like she knows how to wield a weapon. It's sexy *and* intriguing.

"Oh. Sorry, I didn't notice. I was distracted by the beauty in the room." Ah fuck. I glower. What the fuck did I say that for? My brain can't decide if it wants to fuck with her or be genuine, and now I'm coming off like some deranged sociopath. *Pick a path, Baxter. Fuck her to fuck with Cordelia or try to make a meaningful connection for once in your sorry life.*

I sigh. I guess I'll pick the first path. It's a damn sight easier. And it'll at least end in sex. I need to be more charming, less creepy, but this girl is looking like a hard sell. There's a look in her eyes that says she isn't going to fall for any of my usual bullshit, and I might just have to try harder with this one. I'm surprised. I'm not used to trying, and I'm certainly not used to high society girls posing any sort of a challenge. Although this one seems as far from high society as it's possible to get. Is she even Cordelia's granddaughter? I don't see any resemblance.

"Well, I'm starving," she says, drawing me from my thoughts. "So if you could begin, I'll be able to get my main course sooner. I hope it's more substantial than whatever this fairy food is."

"Fairy food?" Again, I want to laugh. My lips twitch and I don't remember the last time I had so little control over my own damn body. My dick bobs in agreement and I mentally tell it to calm the fuck down too.

She stares pointedly at my plate, ignoring me until I get the hint and pick up my fork to begin.

"Yes, fairy food. All pretty and dainty. Portion size only big enough to fill a fairy."

I can't help but snort in amusement, picking up the tiny morsel from my plate and popping it into my mouth in one go. She's right of course, but usually chicks dig this fancy ass shit. Does this one even care that she's eating food created by the most decorated celebrity chef in the world? Obviously not, because if he could hear the way she's derisively describing his food, his ego would be beyond wounded.

I decide that I definitely like her. She was born into this world and she doesn't fit at all. But rather than try to be fake, she's giving everyone the finger. Like me.

"This is a five hour, twelve-course tasting menu. The portion sizes have to be small; otherwise you'd pop." I laugh again easily. There's a...lightness in my chest I've not felt in a long while. I get something similar around Amelie but to a lesser extent. There's always some concern there, knowing how much danger she's in, and having to deal with my wanting to protect her and not just because I'm paid to.

No, this girl makes me feel...happy? I'm not sure. Am I capable of that emotion? Fucking makes me feel good. Plotting too. Revenge, killing, torturing all make me feel sated. But happy? That's a new one for me.

"Wait! What? Five hours?"

"At least." I smirk, enjoying the clear discomfort on her face when she realises that she'll be stuck here with me for a while yet. I'm pretty sure she planned to eat and run, but it gives me time to seduce her course by course. They say the way to a man's heart is through his stomach. I never understood that. I eat to keep my body functioning. But maybe the way to a woman's heart is through food too? I have no idea. In the past it seemed to be through my name and bank balance but this girl doesn't seem that way inclined.

"I'd rather have a steak and ice cream," she blurts out, just as the servers enter to take away our plates. There's a look of horror on everyone's faces and my shoulders shake. Uh-oh, she's in trouble now when the chef finds out.

When we're alone again, we sit in silence. She seems uncomfortable, sighing and fidgeting. I don't mind; every time she wiggles, her dress slides a little further up her thighs. I wonder what colour her underwear is.

"What do you do?" she breaks the silence.

"I'm about to graduate from university." I appreciate the thoughtfulness of her question. Most people assume I don't do anything, just sit around waiting for Grandfather to die so that I can start blowing his legacy on booze and breasts, or pills and pussy.

"Oh, how old are you then? I thought you were my age." She

looks at me with curiosity. Damn. I should have lied. This is going to lead to more questions.

"I'm older," I reply flatly, hoping to shut her down.

"What do you read?" she digs. It's like she can sense I don't want to go down this line of questioning, and is trying to provoke me.

Is she stupid? I've killed guys for less. I level her with a hard look.

"Books."

"Funny."

"My degree's in business management." I sigh. Here we go...

"Oh, where from?"

"Knox Academy." The fucking school of the bastard devil. It stole my soul in exchange for a tuition I never even asked for.

"I've never heard of it." She pulls a face.

"You wouldn't have." Nice girl like her at a school for people like me? Ha. As if. Amelie barely fits in. She thinks she's so badass but she didn't even kill that guy. She's too kind, her heart's too big, she's taking the rap for that twat back home. Wouldn't mind spilling a little of his blood.

Actually though, looking more closely at the girl in front of me, I can see she has something about her. There's mettle there. Knox would eat her alive, sure, but she's clearly not some society bimbo like I first assumed.

"Ooooh is it like some super-secret posh school for the rich? Or is it a spy school?"

"Something like that," I evade.

"Let me guess; you're going to manage a business with that degree?"

"Wow, you're so clever I can't believe you've not graduated

early…" I drawl back sarcastically. She's touched a nerve. "Yes I'm going to run businesses, my grandfather's for one."

If I live that long. I'm still not sure how to get out of The Order. When Grandfather first collected me and word got back that I was 'missing', I thought it would be the perfect opportunity to disappear, but my damn curiosity got the better of me and I called Frost. He has to be the reason Amelie found me, and if she knows I'm alive, the Knox brothers will know I'm alive, and so will The Order.

Which means I'm dead.

"Well, that's stupid," she says, pulling a face.

"Why?" I scowl.

"Because what idiot would be stupid enough to hand over the reins of their company to a kid fresh out of school with no practical business experience?" My jaw hangs in shock. I'm so astonished by the brazen way she speaks her mind, that I'm half tempted to spill my secrets just to shut her up. She wants experience? If only she knew what I've done.

"Why does a piece of paper that says you read a few books and wrote a few essays make you more qualified to run an actual business than say, people who have decades of experience?"

She swallows nervously at the look I give her – like I'd love nothing more than to cause her pain and fuck her senseless right now. I quickly try to school my expression, but I know she catches it because her eyes harden in defiance.

"Interesting idea," is all I say, too enraged to say more. She's so close to being bent over the table and taught to hold her goddamn tongue.

Once again, the doors open, and the next course is served. I have a pretty good idea what's coming and sure enough, the chef doesn't disappoint. She looks down at her plate, lip already curling in a disapproving sneer when she blinks in shock.

Our plates are both full to the brim with steak and chips. I can practically see her mouth watering as the server passes her a steak knife.

"Now this is more like it!" she exclaims, digging straight in, excited.

"Glad you're happy."

"Please tell me this is it instead of another ten courses?"

"Nine. You have ice cream for dessert." I grin. Her happiness is infectious.

"Awesome!"

"Do you really love steak and ice cream that much, or do you just want out of here quicker?"

"A little of one, a lot of the other."

I laugh at her joke and join her, eating in silence. I enjoy the steak almost as much as the view and the company.

After dinner, as she starts on her dessert, I change seats and sit beside the girl. She doesn't say anything but I can tell from the tense set of her shoulders that she's not happy.

I drop my hand to her thigh.

"What the fuck?" She growls, dropping her spoon and glowering.

"What?" I ask coldly. She's not behaving like normal girls do, so maybe she needs a not so subtle reminder of how this is going to work. "I got you the dinner that you wanted, so why don't you show me how grateful you are?"

My voice is steel. My eyes, ice. The weight of my intention presses down heavily on her bare skin. She doesn't reply, move, react in any way.

"No, thanks. I'm taken," she eventually says stiffly.

"I don't see a ring." I smirk.

She waves her hand in front of my face, and I laugh again. Her grandmother could have given her that ring. It means nothing to me.

"It's on the wrong hand, honey." I don't like the taste of that term of endearment on my tongue. It doesn't suit her at all. This girl isn't sweet.

"Means the same thing though. I'm taken. And not interested."

"Is that so?" I drawl. "Then why haven't you moved my hand?"

I'm more than a little smug as she glances down at where my hand is still resting on her leg. Even now she makes no move to remove it.

Trying to provoke her further, I start to lightly stroke and work my way higher. Then I squeeze the soft skin in my grip.

She snaps.

Her hand shoots out and grabs something. She moves with such lightning fast reflexes, I can't even process what it is. Fiery pain explodes through the back of my hand and I howl in pain. It's the shock that does it. I've sustained far worse with barely a sigh passing my lips before now.

It turns out to be her steak knife which she has driven through my flesh. My dick springs to fucking attention like a goddamn masochist soldier reporting for duty.

She shoots to her feet, the chair toppling over, and rushes to the door. I grab the nearest napkin and attempt to staunch the blood. Before she can reach for the handle, the doors fly open, and both of our grandparents are taking in the scene with horrified looks on their faces.

"What's going on?" My grandfather demands.

"Is everything okay?"

"No, it's not! Baxter's had a little accident," she says with a falsely sweet little smile.

An accident? Really?! How the hell would I accidentally stab myself with a steak knife during a dessert course?! How the hell am I going to explain that one?!

I purse my lips and glower at her, but I won't say anything. The Order taught me better than that.

"I think he might need stitches."

No fucking shit, darling! Of course I'll need bloody stitches! I'm pissing blood everywhere. I have a steak knife still stuck in my hand!

"I have to go, I'm so sorry, but if I see blood I'll faint."

Yeah I call bullshit on that, I think, as she rushes past our grandparents.

"Raven wait!" Cordelia calls, turning to grimace apologetically at Grandfather. "I'm so sorry, Dicky, I have to make sure she's alright." Is she kidding me right now? I'm the one who just got fucking stabbed!

I shift in my seat, subtly trying to rearrange my pants. I'm harder than steel. That girl looks like she loves to bathe in the blood of her enemies. Holy fuck. I think I just fell in love.

Baxter: I need help.

Message delivered

Baxter: Amelie, are you there?

Message delivered

Baxter: I need some friendly advice.

Message delivered

Amelie: Pretty sure you need friends for that...

Message delivered

Baxter: Just one. Will you be my one and only?

Message delivered

Chapter Eleven

Amelie

The buzz of an incoming call wakes me from my slumber. Panic leaps into my throat as I hit answer without checking the caller display. My mind immediately jumps to Onyx and then Baxter. Are they okay?

"Come take care of me," a voice whines down the line.

"Fuck off, Kalen," I snap. "It's the middle of the goddamn night."

"I can't sleep."

"Boo-hoo, you shouldn't have had so much sugar. I thought Sawyer or Slate was calling to say something had happened to Onyx. Or Baxter."

"You really care about him don't you?" he says in a quiet voice.

"I care about all of you," I reply simply.

"Good. Then come care for me."

"Goodnight, Kalen." I sigh.

"Wait! I just got beat up by your brother. The least you can do is nurse me back to health."

"If you need medical assistance after two punches to the gut, your brothers are going to tear you a new one once we're home and they find out about this."

"Just come cuddle me!" he whines. "I'm lonely."

"Nope. Your bed is too small."

"Then let me come get in yours. I'll be really quiet."

"Kalen, you couldn't be quiet if your life depended on it," I scold him. A cuddle would be nice though. I'm quiet for a moment and then I have an idea. "Meet me outside in ten minutes. Bring a blanket!"

I hang up and leave my room. I decide not to be sneaky about it, if anyone 'catches' me I'll just say I'm heading to the kitchen to grab a drink. Kalen's on his own. If he gets busted, it's up to him to come up with an excuse.

Luckily, no one disturbs me and I'm able to slip out the back door to the garden. Of course the jumping castle is still inflated. The thing is so huge it took over half an hour to blow up and Kalen convinced Chelsea to leave it up over night so that the kids could have one last bounce in the morning before the guy collects it. At least I don't need to worry about suddenly turning the power on and waking everyone.

I cross the grass barefoot and climb into the giant inflatable, lighting my way with my phone and then passing the time while I wait for Kalen by playing a game. I idly wonder what time it is back in the UK, and wherever Baxter is, and I contemplate reaching out.

When all the excitement of the day is done, and I'm alone in my bed at night left with just my thoughts and the horrible churning 'what if' scenarios going around and around in my mind, it gets hard to breathe. I feel like I made a mistake coming here, even though during the day when I'm surrounded by friends and family it's a soothing balm to my soul, I should never have left Onyx.

Not only that, but I have bridges to build with Slate too. I treated him terribly the last few weeks, pushing him away because I couldn't bear for him to be okay while Onyx wasn't. Now that Onyx is going to be okay, I feel worse than ever. I should have kept my family close, not pushed them away. But flight or fight has always been my downfall. I'm just grateful that the boys didn't give up on me, and dragged me back to face reality. Even if I was kicking and screaming the whole time.

"What are you planning, dear sis?" Kalen startles me, pushing his head through the entrance to the jumping castle and grinning at me maniacally in the torch light.

"Shush!" I chastise him, even though he wasn't loud, he just scared me. "Get in here before my brother looks out of the window and sees you!"

"I think you mean our brother, sis," he replies as he climbs in and joins me. He has the torch on his phone switched on and in his free hand he's holding a couple of blankets.

"I'm not your damn sister, Kalen." I sigh but I'm biting back a smile. I love that he was the first to accept me into their weird fucked up family. I love that even though Laura isn't my mum, he still considers me family. At least he dropped the idea of me being his future wife. Of course he'd prefer the excitement of potential incest over marriage. He's incorrigible.

"No, but if Laura marries Monty, Aadi will be my brother. Do you think he'll get matching bro tattoos with me?" I snort. Aadi would kick his head in if he tried.

"Try him and see." I chuckle at the mental image and then

sober. "Besides, Laura and Monty will happen over my dead body."

"I expect Laura would probably capitalise on your funeral. What an excellent way to make it all about her by getting hitched on your grave."

I shudder at his joke. I despise that woman but I could see her wearing white to my wake and making it all about her like Kalen says. She's a piece of work.

I never thought I could hate her more than I did when she abused and then abandoned me, but I was still young and desperate for love. I guess I still am, I've just learnt that it can be found in the arms of others. However, finding out that she isn't really my mum and that there really was no reason for the sick things she used to do to me, has somehow made it worse. I vow revenge. I will use whatever resources The Order have at their disposal to bring her down and make her pay. For good.

"You're plotting, sis. Do share. You know I love to fuck shit up. I like to consider myself the king shenanigator."

"Just thinking about Laura. What the hell is a shenanigator?"

"It's a person who instigates shenanigans. They're my speciality. You dragged me out here in the middle of the night to plan a murder?"

"Does that turn you on?" I smirk. I did not drag him out here to plan a murder, no matter how appealing that might be. I'm on holiday and if I'm not allowed to call and fly home to Onyx on a whim, I'm certainly not thinking about The Order and 101 ways to kill a bitch with a paperclip or whatever weird voodoo shit they like to teach.

"No. Why would it?" He frowns at me, completely missing my teasing tone. "Unlike some people who are all into kinky sex and need to be punched in the throat with their leg in a bear trap to be able to come, I'm good with plain old vanilla."

"Kalen, firstly? There's nothing vanilla about your monster cock." He preens at that and it takes all my strength not to slap his big head. "Secondly, planning a murder isn't kinky sex. It's not sex at all."

"Well, are we planning murder or did you drag me out here for kinky sex on a bouncy castle?" he huffs.

"This isn't kinky either," I say, looking around the brightly coloured children's castle. "Inviting an audience to watch us would be kinky. Besides, you were the one whining about needing to be taken care of. Are we doing this or what?"

"Jeez, sis, when you proposition me so enticingly, how could I possibly say no?"

"Just hurry up and get naked before we get caught," I snap impatiently. Honestly, I wish I never answered the damn call now.

"Ah-ha!" He snaps his fingers in triumph. "So you're not as kinky as you like to think you are, otherwise you wouldn't care about being caught."

"When have I ever said I'm kinky, Kalen?" I scowl at him.

"My brothers talk."

"Have I ever said I'm unhappy with the way you and I do things?" I ask.

"Well, no but—"

"But nothing, butthead. I love..." I quickly catch myself and change tack. "I love having sex with all of you for different reasons. You give me something none of them can—"

"Extra inches." He sounds bitter but still looks smug about it. I chuckle.

"That, and the best friendship. I'm not as close to any of them as I am to you. You make me laugh the most. You were the first to accept me, to like me. You're the one who saved me when Onyx…" Again I trail off, unable to go there. "I love our sex. I wouldn't change it for the world."

Kalen smiles at me – a genuine beaming smile that lights up his entire face – and it makes me feel all warm inside. I don't know why he was acting all butthurt but I'm glad I've made him feel better. Without lying. I meant every word.

He leaps at me, grabbing my waist and tackling me to the floor of the jumping castle, where we bounce together and I laugh. Pinning me, he straddles my hips and gazes down at me with love. That warm feeling inside of me grows. I made the right choice. Not just in coming here to Australia with him, but in returning to the UK after I ran away last year. In going back after fleeing when Onyx got hurt. In resolving to forgive them and let go of the anger. In deciding to join The Order.

"Kiss me, you g—" I'm just about to say 'goof' when Kalen descends on me and gives me the sweetest kiss. Even as our lips touch, I can't help the smile that stretches across my face. When he's not making me laugh and getting into mischief, or bragging about his monster cock or winding everyone up, he's actually unbelievably sweet. The size of his heart can rival his ego and his cock for sure.

He distracts me with more kisses, dotting them all over my face like a pecking hen, making me laugh. I try to push him away but he grinds his hips into mine and I gasp. *That* is not playful at all. Kalen gives me a wicked grin, leaning in slowly so that my breath catches. I'm so sure he's going to kiss me properly this time, but at the last second he ducks past my lips and licks the length of my cheek.

"Eww! Kalen!" I whine.

"What's the matter sis?"

"I thought you were going to kiss me."

"I have been. Watch." He returns to his light teasing pecks and I groan.

"Kalen!"

"What?"

"Kiss me!"

"I am!" he snarks. I growl and try to buck him off me, but even as the smallest Knox brother he's incredibly strong. All I succeed in doing is thrusting my crotch up against his. Which he loves. "Tut-tut. Patience, sis."

I sigh and huff in frustration but relax under him. May as well, I'm not going anywhere until he decides to get the hell off me. Besides, playful Kalen is fun, even if he is teasing the hell out of me.

"Kalen, come on."

"What? I'm enjoying myself. It's nice that I don't have to rush. It's not freezing, we're not drunk, we're not pissed at each other, I don't have to share you… I want to do this right."

He returns to kissing me, his hands softly stroking everywhere my skin is bare. It's still hot here, even at night in Queensland, so I was only sleeping in a crop top and shorts. It allows Kalen plenty of places to roam. His touch is so light it's like skimming velvet. He barely makes contact but it still awakens every nerve ending in my body.

It feels like it's been so long since I was touched. Sure, Kalen and I had our thank god Onyx isn't dead fuck, but we didn't really connect. Not like this. This is…so much more.

I squirm under him, needing and wanting more, but he doesn't take a hint. In all honesty, I love what he's doing, I'm just being an impatient greedy bitch.

"Kalen," I complain. He grins at me, sliding his hands under my arms to pull me into a sitting position. From there he spreads a blanket out behind me and peels my shirt over my head, discarding it god knows where. With a gentle shove to my shoulders I'm falling back onto the soft blanket but not before I tangle my fingers in Kalen's hair and bring him down with me. A giggle escapes me and Kalen gives me a one-sided smile which makes my heart flip. He looks so carefree and boyish. It's definitely been too long.

He feathers kisses along my jaw, neck and collarbone, and down onto my bare breasts, all the while I have my fingers tangled in his hair. Thank goodness it's grown back.

"I love your hair. Please don't cut it again."

"I didn't by choice," he murmurs.

I want to ask him what he means but he distracts me by taking my nipple into his mouth and gently rolling it between his teeth. The only thing I'm capable of doing is gasping in surprise. Clutching his head tighter to me, I arch up to him, silently begging for more.

He doesn't give me what I crave though, releasing my now hardened bud with a pop and returning to his teasing caresses. He moves south, hooking his fingers in the waistband of my shorts and pulling them down. Maddeningly, he completely ignores my sex, moving to my ankles and slowly running his tongue up the inside of my leg. My breath catches in anticipation, but he lets me down again.

A frustrated growl escapes me, and I feel rather than see him smile against my skin as he repeats the process on the other leg. I'm contemplating trapping his head between my thighs until he gives me what I want, but for some crazy reason I let him continue driving me wild.

Eventually, when I'm a writhing mess under him, he gets the hint.

"Fuck, you're so tight sis."

"Not...your...damn...sister!" I pant out as he slowly slides one, two, three fingers into me and steals my ability to function.

"Mmmmhmmm, why are you so wet then if you don't love me calling you that?"

"Dick."

"Monster cock baby, monster cock."

"Gimme," is all I can manage.

"Patience."

He continues to pump his fingers into me at an agonisingly slow pace, but I feel so full and stretched that I don't mind. It doesn't take long for my muscles to tighten and my legs to begin that tell-tale tremble that indicates how close to losing control I really am.

"Kalen, please."

"I don't think I'm gonna let you come."

"What!? No! Why?!"

"Maybe if you ask nicely."

"Kalen, please! Please let me come."

"Brother."

"What?"

"Call me brother and I'll let you come."

"Noooooo," I groan, throwing my arm over my eyes. I'm so close. This can't be happening.

He cackles wickedly and circles my clit with his tongue, eliciting a helpless whimper from me.

"Kalen..."

"No can do sis."

I groan again, my cheeks on fire. I *can't*. But...I need to come. And there's no one around to hear me, right? I can deny it later if Kalen ever mentions it again.

"Tick tock, sis. My hand's getting tired, I might have to stop—"

"Don't you dare!" I snap. He sniggers. Absolute bastard.

"Please, let me come...brother," I add in the tiniest voice that's barely above a whisper.

"Fuck yeah, you almost make me come in my pants when you say that!" Kalen crows. I keep my hands over my face, mortified beyond all belief and convinced I'll never be able to look him or Aadi, my actual brother, in the eye ever again.

"I hate you," I groan.

But it doesn't matter, because it does the trick. Kalen speeds up, his fingers keeping time with his tongue which finally, *finally* makes contact with my clit. With a muffled shout, I clamp down around him and earn my release. *Holy fuck.*

Kalen grins at me, my juices glistening on his face, and moves back up my body. I don't even care when he kisses me and I taste myself on his tongue. It's fucking hot and I taste good. I kiss him deeper, desperate for more, and this time he groans into my mouth while pressing his huge cock against my opening.

"Fuck, I don't think I've ever seen anyone come so hard."

"Maybe you can rectify that. Fuck me, Kalen."

Thankfully, I don't have to ask twice. Kalen's right, I'm fucking soaked. So thanks to that and his three finger ministrations, he slides in easily. I still feel uncomfortably full though.

As he starts to move his hips, oh so slowly, all thoughts of discomfort flee my mind. He kisses me deeply and drags his body along mine in a way which creates delicious friction against my already sensitive skin. I lose myself in him for a moment but when I realise that he has no plans to change tempo, I break away from our kiss.

"Kalen," I complain on another whine. "What the fuck are you doing?"

"Fucking you."

"This isn't fucking."

"I'm making sw—"

"I swear to god if you even dream of finishing that sentence, I'll snap your dick off!"

"I can't really *do* more. It's too…squidgy," he replies. I smirk at him.

"Hey, it's okay. It's late. And it happens to everyone," I tease.

"The bouncy castle, moron. I can't get a grip. It's frustrating as fuck."

"You're telling me."

"Whose stupid idea was this anyway? You should have just let me come into your room."

"With my family right next door?"

"You could have been quiet."

"Fat chance. Although if I knew you were going to fuck me like a soggy sponge I could have risked it."

"Right, that's it," he snaps, withdrawing and moving away from me. I instantly feel bereft. "Get up."

He tugs my hand to pull me up, then flips me over so that I'm on all fours. Ah fuck. I barely survived this position with him last time.

A loud crack rings out as he lands a stinging blow to my right ass cheek and I yelp in surprise. That was most definitely unexpected. Before I can yell at him for it though, he's gripping my hips and slamming into me with such force I'm almost knocked over.

"Fuck!" I hiss as I push back against him and eagerly meet his thrusts. "Damn, that feels good."

"*You* feel damn good," Kalen pants out as he finally manages to build some momentum, falling into a bruising, punishing rhythm.

Like this, it doesn't take long at all for me to tumble over the edge again, clamping down around him and triggering his orgasm with my own. I collapse forward onto the jumping castle, not caring that the blanket has got all rucked up. Kalen follows, covering my body as he tries to catch his breath.

"Get off me, you great lump," I complain.

"I was pretty great, wasn't I?" I can hear the smugness in his tone without even needing to see his annoying face.

"Ugh. You're so…" Nope. I have no words.

"Wow fucked speechless. I *am* good!"

I huff but it turns into a wince as he withdraws and I'm left feeling so empty. Kalen presses something against me, and when I glance over my shoulder I see it's his shirt. Which is really sweet, but I can't exactly put that in the wash for Chelsea to clean up. And I don't particularly want it hanging around in his suitcase until we go home. Damn.

"We should head back inside," Kalen tells me. I don't want to make his big head even bigger but there's no way I can move just yet. My bones have liquefied. I'm jelly.

"Umm, yeah. Should probably sneak in separately though. You go ahead and I'll follow in a few."

"You sure? Here's your clothes." He hands them to me as I flip onto my back and just about manage to sit up. I catch them and thank him, slowly pulling them on and passing him back his shirt.

"So...I'll see you in the morning then?" Kalen asks awkwardly.

"Yeah." I bite my lip. Why does this feel so weird? What do I say? Kalen sighs.

"I wish I could sleep in your bed with you."

I nod at him.

He grabs the blankets and with one last indecipherable look at me, disappears back towards the house. I locate my phone and check the time, deciding to wait five minutes. I can grab that drink from the kitchen on the way back in.

When my time's up, I hurry through the garden to the house, stopping for a glass of water before moving upstairs. The house is quiet and I breathe a sigh of relief as I slip back into my bed, undetected.

I'm just relaxing back, melting into my mattress, when my bedroom door opens and my heart flies into my throat.

"I had to say goodnight properly," Kalen whispers, rushing across the room to kiss me deeply. "I love you, Amelie."

I blink and he's gone as fast as he appeared, the warmth on my lips the only evidence I didn't just dream his fleeting visit. A small smile plays on my face as I think about Kalen's call. I started the night frustrated with him for waking me up. But it was totally worth it.

Amelie: Okay, shoot. You may have won me over a little bit.

Message delivered

Baxter: Seriously? How? What did I do?

Message delivered

Amelie: Erm, that one and only stuff?!

Message delivered

Baxter: Really? Does that shit work?

Message delivered

Amelie: Goodbye Baxter Reginald Branson.

Message delivered

Baxter: Lol! Not even close!

Message delivered

Chapter Twelve

Baxter

I did need stitches. Twenty in fact. Ten on the back of my hand and another ten on the palm. The cut was small of course, even though she drove the knife right through with surprising strength, but my grandfather only employs the best, and so an expert surgeon was on standby to stitch me up. Pretty sure I could have done it myself, but this way the scarring will be minimal. Just like that cut to Kalen's cheek. Damn boy is too pretty for his own good. I don't mind a scar or two. I'll happily wear them as badges of honour. Unlike Slate who prefers to keep his shame hidden.

I can't help but wonder what state I'll find Onyx in when I go back home. I had planned to wait out the rest of the break here on the island, but I find myself fired up and restless to get moving. I have so many questions I want to find the answers to now, a purpose I didn't have before.

Raven's words keep ringing in my ears too. About my lack of business experience. I've barely been trying in my studies. To begin with, I was keen to impress Daddy Knox, but once I understood that he was just using me, I stopped trying. So long as I was doing what he wanted, he would let my grades slide. But...I'm due to leave Knox in a few short months. And if I really want to stand on my own two feet away from The Order (assuming they let me live long enough to try) I'm going to need an actual degree to be able to do that. Not just a token slip of paper with a bachelors in business management scrawled on it by Monty. If it's not too late, I want to try. I want to earn that right to take over the reins of my grandfather's company.

Which is another reason to head home. I have exams after the break. Exams which I'd better start studying for. I'm not foolish enough to think I can turn around nearly four years of not giving a fuck in a matter of weeks, but if I put *some* sort of effort in, at least I won't be ashamed or feel like a total fraud come graduation day.

I manage to intercept Grandfather on his own at breakfast.

"Can we talk?" I ask. He sighs and looks at me wearily.

"What is it, Baxter?"

"Where's Cu-Cordelia?" I ask in the most civil tone I can manage. I don't give a fuck, I just want to make sure that she isn't going to interrupt us.

"She's having breakfast with Charlotte. Raven. Damn it."

"You know, that's weird," I point out.

"Having breakfast with your grandchild is not weird, Baxter."

"Obviously," I drawl, heavy on the sarcasm. "We're doing it now and this isn't strange at all. What I meant was, it's weird how you keep getting her name wrong. What's with that?"

"She changed her name. It happens. It's just taking a little getting used to."

"I didn't think you'd met before," I let slip before realising that he never told me that, I simply deduced as much from spying on their first meeting.

"Cordelia and I have been in each other's lives for a very long time. Of course I know all about her family and she knows about mine. I may not have met Raven before now, but I know a lot about her."

"And does she know about your life, not just your family?"

"Of course."

"Even The Order?"

"Don't be ridiculous, Baxter. There are some things even more sacred than love."

I scoff at that. Both at the suggestion that he loves Cuntdelia and at his insistence that The Order and its secrets are important.

"Anyway, I want to talk to you about my degree…" I begin before filling him in on my plans. He seems surprised but once he gets over the initial shock of my suggestion, he listens attentively and nods along.

"I think that is an excellent idea. I won't make you start from the very bottom in my company to work your way up though, I think an entry level management position will do. You are a Branson after all. We have standards to maintain. But yes, I think getting some practical business experience would be good for you, and it will definitely alleviate my concerns about handing over the reins to you."

I smile at him, a genuine smile, and he returns it with warmth before clapping me on the back.

"Well done. I don't know what made you think of this, but I'm proud of you, Baxter."

"Well, that's the other thing," I say. "I have exams in a few weeks' time so I think it's time I stop moping and catch a flight back home. I have some studying to do."

For a second the old man looks like he might keel over with the shock and I worry that it was a step too far but then his face breaks out into a beaming grin and he rushes off to have the private plane readied for me.

Good. He doesn't need to know that it's partially a ruse. I mean, Raven was right and I do want to do better, but it will also keep him from nagging me about taking a more active role in The Order. Plus, with going home early, I can start investigating what's going on.

My phone rings and I answer the call when I see it's my grandfather, already calling with an update about the plane no doubt.

"Plane will be ready to go by morning. Is that okay?"

"It's perfect. Thank you, Grandfather."

Amelie: I've decided, it has to be really embarrassing.

Message delivered

Baxter: What does? What are you on about?

Message delivered

Amelie: Your middle name, obviously. It has to be pretty bad, why else would you have it wiped from all the records?

Message delivered

Baxter: And you think there's a name worse than Reginald?

Message delivered

Amelie: Stanley...Wilson...Manson...Yugo...

Message delivered

Baxter: Did you hit your head in the explosion?

Message delivered

Amelie: OMG! Please don't tell me your middle name also begins with B!

Message delivered

Baxter: There's nothing wrong with alliterative names...

Message delivered

Amelie: O. M. G. It totally is. That narrows it down some...

Message delivered

Chapter Thirteen

Amelie

"Bugger off, Kalen!" I moan what feels like moments later when the door slowly creaks open.

"I'm surprised he's not in your bed with you," a bitter voice sounds out. My eyes fly open in panic.

"Smalls!" I sit bolt upright and clutch the covers to my chin. "What time is it?"

"Early. We're the only ones up."

"Are you okay? Did something happen?" I frown. Why is he waking me up so early? I feel like I *just* closed my eyes. We're supposed to be going to the beach today and it'll be hell on so little sleep. Kalen isn't going to let me doze in the sun, he'll want to play in the ocean and be his usual hyperactive self.

"No. I'm not okay."

"What is it?" I ask, concern filling my eyes. I scoot over in the bed to make room for him and pat the mattress beside me. Wordlessly, Smalls slides in and lays his head on my pillow. I copy, turning onto my side so that I can face him. We're so close our noses are almost touching.

"What happened?" I repeat on a whisper.

"I saw you. With *him*. Last night." The cover, pulled up to my ear, trembles lightly under Smalls' barely suppressed anger. Is he...jealous?

"Smalls—"

"Amelie, I'm so sorry."

"What? Why?" I blink, surprised by his sudden change of topic.

"Where do I start? I should never have pushed you away. I shouldn't have said we can't be happy together. We can make us work. I can talk to your dad and Aadi, I'm sure they will...."

"Smalls..." I warn, I thought we sorted this out, he seriously isn't doing this right now.

"No. Let me finish, babygirl! Ah...fuck it... "

He doesn't finish. He plants his lips against mine and my eyes nearly pop out of my head. Oh my god. I pull away at the same time as my hands find his chest and push.

"No no no no no. I can't do this with you!"

"Amelie, please—"

"No. You were right last time. This...us...it isn't right. It isn't meant to be like this."

"But I love you."

"And I love you. I always will but—"

"No. No buts. Listen, come home. I'll go to the police and tell them it was me. We can be together if you wait until I'm out of prison. Wait for me, babygirl. Be mine."

"I can't do that, Smalls." I sigh at the painful twist in my heart. He doesn't mean it. I have no idea what's triggered this desperation in him, but I know it's not his true feelings talking. "It's not that kind of love. And I can't let you throw your life away for me, not when I can't be there waiting for you. I can't love you like that. Like you deserve."

"But you can love *him* like that?"

I nod.

"And the others?"

"Smalls—"

"How? How Amelie!? How can you love four of them but not have any room for me?!"

"You know you're not good at sharing," I say softly, a sad smile tugging at my lips. How can I make this better? How do I ease his pain?

"For you I could."

"You'd hate it. I'd make you miserable and I can't do that."

"You should give me a chance. It's up to me to decide if I want to—"

"It's up to me too. And I just…" I take a deep breath, aware that I'm about to rip his heart out. But knowing that ultimately, I have to. "I just don't feel that way about you."

He hisses in pain, his face falling. Climbing out of my bed, he storms for the door. He yanks it open and stares at me coldly for a moment.

"You're a real piece of work, Amelie."

The door slams shut and my heart thunders in my chest. He doesn't mean it. He doesn't love me. He… Tears stream down my face. This is *not* how I saw this vacation going at all.

I wait for Smalls to come back and say he didn't mean it, that he was just having a moment, but it doesn't happen. He finally said all the things I've always wanted to hear but now things have changed. The Knox brothers have wormed their way into my heart and each one makes me feel things I never knew I could feel. It made me realise that what I felt for Smalls was puppy love; he protected me and made me feel safe, and I clung to that for a long time.

My bedroom door swings open and for a split second I think it's going to be Smalls but Kalen comes barrelling into the room and jumps onto the bed, a huge smile plastered on his face.

"Guess what?!" he asks. I shake my head. Something has made him super happy this morning, so he certainly hasn't run into Smalls.

"You're mad and I'm not," I throw back. He looks at me like I have lost my mind.

"No, Chelsea has changed our plans for today. She has borrowed someone named Linda's minivan." I try to keep up with how fast he is talking. "And we are all going to the zoo! Can you believe it?! They have kangaroos at the zoo! And you know how disappointed I was when I found out you don't keep them as pets!"

I laugh at his enthusiasm. We have been to Australia Zoo a million times, Chelsea loves it. I think she secretly had a crush on Steve Irwin growing up.

"We have to meet downstairs in half an hour, so get dressed." With that he kisses my lips and pushes himself up on the bed and races back downstairs.

Getting up, I check my phone. I have a few texts from Baxter, a couple from Elsie, Slate and Sawyer. One from Onyx catches my eye.

Onyx: *I miss you. When are you coming back?*

I hit call and walk over to my door and close it. Kalen has said since I'm here on holiday I need to not keep checking up on Onyx, but he needs me.

"Hey," he says, answering just as the call would have

connected to the answering machine.

"Were you working out?" I ask. He is still on strict orders to take it easy.

"Just a small jog, it's the only thing that takes my mind off things."

"Are you still having nightmares?" I know Onyx, he takes everything on his shoulders, what happened to Slate as a child has always weighed him down, and now this.

"I keep dreaming that they come back and take you away from me... As much as it kills me to say this, I should have listened to Branson."

"What was that? I didn't quite hear you," I joke. Baxter is going to get a kick out of this when I text him back.

"I'm being dead serious Amelie. He didn't want you in; he knew something like this would happen. The Order is no place for women."

"You take that back! Women can do exactly what men can. The difference in this situation is that you have feelings for me, you feel responsible for me in some way, but so help me if you get in the way of Sawyer's plans, I will kill you myself. That old fool doesn't get to try to take me down over his hurt male pride and get away with it."

"I'm sorry. We dragged you into this lifestyle and it's for life, Amelie. You can't walk away. We didn't quite grasp that when we joined, and you're poised to take over and rule, that's a lot more to handle."

"I know. And we'll all deal with it together, as a unit."

He sighs, hopefully realising I'm right.

A loud bang has me jumping round to face the door.

"Amelie, what was that?! Amelie! Answer me!"

"What the fuck, Kalen?!" I stammer, my heart still lodged in my throat. He walks calmly around the bed and takes the phone from my hand.

"Sucks to be you, douche," Kalen says with a smirk before hanging up the phone. He takes a big step towards me.

"Who dobbed me in? It was Sawyer wasn't it? Once a teacher, always a teacher. Damn snitch."

"Doesn't matter. You're supposed to be enjoying your holiday."

How am I supposed to enjoy myself? Onyx is still not 100 percent. I miss Marshmallow. I miss Elsie, Slate and Sawyer...and even bloody Frost and Jasper! And to top it off Smalls is being weird.

"Okay, bossy britches, get out so I can get dressed."

He willingly leaves, and I throw on something comfy. Knowing Chelsea, she has the entire day mapped out and we all need to make sure we wear the appropriate clothing and shoes. One time, we learned the hard way when we all wore thongs. I'm not sure if Smalls or I had the worst sunburn on our feet.

Traipsing downstairs, I see straight away that Chelsea and Kalen are equally excited. My father is packing an Esky, Smalls is on the sofa looking at his phone, and Aadi scowls at me as I walk into the room.

"This is all your fault," Aadi snaps.

"How is this my fault?"

"You brought *that* home." He points to Kalen and I laugh when I take in what he is wearing. He looks like a stereotypical dad on vacation. He has on khaki shorts, a button up Hawaiian shirt, sneakers with white socks pulled up, a wide brimmed hat, and a bum bag.

"OK. It's my fault." Smalls snorts.

"Do you have an issue?" I snap at him. He looks up, ready to fight back, just as my father walks into the room.

"If you three ruin Chelsea's day, so help me god you will all wish for death. So whatever bullshit you have going on, it stops now and you will all smile and enjoy yourselves until we get home."

"Sure," Aadi agrees.

"Sorry Dad, I think we all just need some coffee," I add.

"Jason?" Dad questions and we all look at Smalls.

"It's all sweet over here," he says, avoiding eye contact with me.

"Good," my father snaps. "Get your asses in the bloody minivan."

We all stand and make our way to the car, Kalen helping my father carry the Esky. Aadi and Smalls take the first seats in the van and Kalen and I have to take the back. Chelsea even gives Kalen control of the music and we end up listening to Chelsea's Blondie playlist. *'Heart of Glass'* spills through the car, Smalls groans and puts his headphones in and Aadi follows suit. I don't blame them, both Kalen and Chelsea sing very off key, but the smiles are well worth it.

🖤 🖤 🖤

Two hours, and one pee stop later, we arrive at Australia Zoo. Kalen is buzzing with excitement, taking in everything around him.

"Take a picture of me in front of the sign?" Kalen asks, thrusting his phone at me. "Make sure you take a few so I have options to put online." He races into position. I peek a glance at Smalls, still hurt he won't look at me. He shakes his head at Kalen and I flip him off. Aadi gives us a serious look, as if to say 'knock it off'.

We take our time exploring, watching Kalen's face light up at each enclosure, taking photos of all the animals. I must admit bringing Kalen here was a fantastic idea, even better than when we brought Chelsea's niece.

Dad and Chelsea walk hand in hand, while Aadi and Smalls trail behind talking amongst themselves. I hang back and wait, hoping to talk to Aadi. Small notices and walks away.

"Hey, sis." I cringe. I knew letting Kalen say it would come back to bite me on the ass. "What's going on between you and the big man?"

"You don't want to know, it could result in a few deaths and I can't have any more of that on my conscience." I laugh nervously because Aadi would slaughter Smalls for wanting me, Kalen for sleeping with me, and me for getting caught.

"I want to ask you a favour," I murmur nervously, glancing over at Kalen who is running for the kids' zoo.

"You know I would do anything for you," he says, throwing his arm over my shoulder pulling me close as we walk together.

"Even make friends with Kalen?" A small smirk pulls at his lips.

"You want a favour and you are willing to use it on one of your boyfriends?" I nod.

"How does that whole dynamic work anyway? Do you, like, split days?"

I laugh. I wondered how long until he would ask. "Nah, we prefer gang bangs," I quip. He stops dead in his tracks, holding me back with him. "Kidding, twin sandwiches aren't bad though." His jaw ticks with anger.

"I'm sorry I asked."

I lose it and laughter escapes me.

"They make me happy. And to answer your earlier question, that is what Smalls is struggling with. I know you don't approve, but we had something between us for years and fighting it was hard. My heart broke splinter by splinter over the years. And now we are moving on, cutting those ties fucking sucks." Aadi and I stop walking. Kalen's and Chelsea's laughter seeps out of the kiddie area.

Aadi pulls me tight into his arms and rests his chin on my head. "I will talk to him, the thought of anyone defiling my little sister makes me murderous, but you're a big girl now and as for Crack Barbie inside, I promise I will make an effort to get to know him. I will even take him out and show him the town...Rossi style."

I groan. Show him the town means taking him to some guy's 'crib' and getting wasted while actual crack whores try to rub themselves on any willing dumb fuck, ones so wasted they're not afraid of catching herpes.

"Thank you. As far as big brothers go, you're pretty cool."

Aadi shoves me away playfully. "Let's go rescue Dad from that insanity."

The rest of the day flies by in a blur of Kalen running around like a squirrel on crack, which was eventful in the kangaroo enclosure. He tried to take a selfie with one that wasn't as enthusiastic as he was. Now he can add kangaroos to his ever-growing list of phobias. A busted lip from being headbutted by a kangaroo should be a good story he can tell his grandkids.

Baxter: What's this thing that thumps inside your chest?

Message delivered

Amelie: A heart? Did you purchase one on the black market?

Message delivered

Baxter: Maybe I did.

Message delivered

Amelie: You will never guess what Onyx just told me!

Message delivered

Baxter: Are you going to tell me? I'm dying from anticipation over here…

Message delivered

Baxter: I hope you could hear the sarcasm in my last text.

Message delivered

Amelie: Fine! I won't tell you.

Message delivered

Baxter: Spit it out, you know you want to.

Message delivered

Amelie: Fine! He said he should have listened to you.

Message delivered

Baxter: Prepare for the apocalypse because Hell just froze over.

Message delivered

Amelie: That's what I said! LOL!

Message delivered

Chapter Fourteen

Baxter

I have some time to kill before my flight tomorrow and what better way to spend it than keeping an eye on my newest obsession?

She's left on her own far too much. I don't like it. Some people – myself included – prefer their own company to being around others. I know that whenever I used to have to play nice with the Knox family I always needed days alone afterward to recover from their company. But this girl? Raven? She seems to hate being alone. Whenever I watch her, which is to say all the fucking time, she seems agitated and restless. I'm pretty sure she's running from something, but that she's...haunted, too.

I mean, many would consider this isle of my grandfather's a literal paradise, but she seems immune to both my charms and the charms of the island. She doesn't take pleasure in being surrounded by the finest things money can buy, nor does she seem to appreciate or take enjoyment from the natural beauty that surrounds her.

She seems...numb.

Every time I lay eyes on her, she confounds me. There are so many mysteries to pick apart and uncover. How can so much pain be wrapped up in such pretty packaging? Though I guess the same could be said of me. Amelie is always telling me she's allowed to appreciate the view that I offer and I know that despite my 'psycho' status at Knox Academy, there are many girls who are still interested. Or maybe it's because of it. I guess I offer the full package: richer than god, famous family… a good-looking bad boy who isn't afraid to carve you up while you're sleeping and bathe in your blood. Who wouldn't be interested?

Raven. Apparently.

Damn I need to find out more about her. I'm not afraid to use any and all connections I have to get intel here. The only thing I won't do is offer up a favour in exchange for that information. Though, I am tempted. Dangerous. Reckless. My favours, my skill set, in the hands of others is not something I take lightly.

I watch like a perverted stalker in the bushes as Raven rises from her sun lounger and crosses towards the swimming pool. At the water's edge her painted toenails curl around the lip of the pool and she stretches for a moment in the late afternoon sun. She has curves, but her golden tanned skin shows how athletic and toned she is. Strong. She looks like a fighter, like she could hold her own. My hand tingles and I glance down at the spot where I'm still wearing a bandage. Yeah, she doesn't *look* like she can hold her own, I *know* she damn well can.

Fuck what I wouldn't give to punish her for that little stunt with the knife! My dick stirs to life in my pants as I watch her execute a dive with grace. Perfect body and perfect form. She glides through the water like she was born there, emerging at the shallow end blinking water from her eyes and pushing her hair from her face into a waterfall cascading down her back. She's closer to me now, though I'm still out of sight, and I can see the sun kissed freckles on her nose that were hidden under the makeup she wore at dinner. She looks even better without that gunk on her face, miles away from the socialite façade her grandmother dressed her in. I itch to know her story. I burn to know her secrets.

As I watch her climb from the pool, tears streaming down her face that are nothing to do with the water, I vow there and then that I *will* uncover every last secret this girl has.

Baxter: What's my best quality?

Message delivered

Amelie: I don't know, princess.

Message delivered

Baxter: I'm being serious, that cunt my grandfather is fucking thinks I have no redeeming qualities!

Mess5thyage delivered

Amelie: Well you're hot, that has to count for something?!

Message delivered

Baxter: Thanks for nothing.

Message delivered

Amelie: You're welcome, Batman.

Message delivered

Baxter: *Insert middle finger emoji*

Message delivered

Amelie: *Insert eggplant emoji*

Message delivered

Baxter: As if you'd know what mine's like. There's no emoji big enough, Robin.

Message delivered

Amelie: Seriously? You know I'm screwing Kalen right? He literally gives the term 'tripod' a whole new meaning.

Message delivered

Baxter: I taught him everything he knows.

Message delivered

Amelie: Holy shit! Did you just make another joke? You don't really strike me as the dick helicoptering sort...

Message delivered

Baxter: You should see me Floss...

Message delivered

Chapter Fifteen

Amelie

Smalls has disappeared, still pissed at me. Kalen and Chelsea are shopping. All I want to do is relax before they get back and Easter explodes throughout the house. Maybe even get a few phone calls in while Kalen is gone. But Dad and Aadi screaming at each other has me running downstairs.

"What the fuck is going on?" I yell, trying to push them apart.

"Nothing sweetheart," my father says, taking a step back and trying to compose himself.

"Jesus Dad, you need to give it up. We don't live here anymore and it's time Amelie knows the truth. All these damn lies are tearing us apart."

I turn to Aadi. What the hell is he talking about?!

"That's because you went to work for your good for nothing grandmother," Dad snaps. He's always hated his mother for as long as I can remember. He rarely speaks about her and I didn't know she even lived close enough for Aadi to work for her.

"So we can't work for her but Amelie can be in The Order? That's so fucking typical."

"You know I had no choice, my hands were tied." Dad is being sincere. I can see it in his eyes.

"There is always a choice! I said no and the reason I went to Grandmother was to protect Amelie. Both Smalls and I did. At least we tried to do something! You just let her go back to that woman who abused her for so many years."

I gasp and shoot Aadi a look. He promised me he would never tell Dad! Dad was always working and I never wanted him to feel guilty.

My father looks at me and opens his mouth to say something but I cut him off. I don't want him to apologise, not when payback is coming really soon.

"Let's back up a second," I say, holding up a finger to Dad and turning to Aadi. "You don't live here anymore? Smalls either?"

He shakes his head.

"No. Dad made us come home when he knew you were coming, so that we could play happy families with you and your energizer bunny boyfriend."

"So where do you live?" I ask.

"Down by The Lakes."

"The fancy part of town? How the hell can you afford that?!"

"By being a gang banger, that's how," my father adds bitterly.

"Dad always forgot to mention his family is loaded."

"From selling drugs and weapons and god knows what else," Dad snaps.

"So no different from what you did in The Order, right? I'm not an idiot Dad, Grandma knows a lot about them, and drugs and weapons are just the tip of the iceberg"

"I'm out, and have been for a long time."

That catches my attention.

"That's a lie. There is no way out. Once you're in it's for life." Guilt washes over my father's face.

"It's more complicated than that. Take a seat and I will explain. Aadi, I think we're done for today. I would appreciate it if you stayed here until your sister leaves but you're grown, so do what you want."

I take a seat and Aadi storms from the room.

"So I need you to explain this to me."

"I can't go into too many details until you are sworn in officially. But you already know The Order works mainly on favours." I nod. "When Laura and I fell in love and she was pregnant with Aadi, I wanted out. I made a deal with the entire board. One I knew I would have to cash in eventually, but I figured it would be a vote in favour of them or to try to convince my mother to play nice. When Monty called I knew they had found out about you. I kept mine and Debbie's relationship a secret because I cheated on Laura and I wasn't proud of that, but Debbie and I always wanted to be together. The Order didn't want that at all because it would have tipped the balance of power if we had a child. Anyway, when he called he said his father had figured it out and you would be in danger. They planned on calling in that favour for you."

"I don't understand."

"Monty and I had a plan. You were supposed to fail the initiation and then he would have found a way to send you home. If Harold got his way and Kalen took over – so that a Knox ruled – you would have been safe. Aadi was supposed to take the Rossi seat on the board when the time came, but he is stubborn and refuses to be part of this."

"Why did you never tell me about Debbie?"

"Laura made me swear not to at the start, and the older you got the harder it became. I wish things were different but they're not."

"Harold isn't a good person. I knew if he found out about you, he would want you dead. My best bet was to make a deal with Monty to keep you safe and he assured me that you would be, so long as his father got his own way."

"And did you or Monty read the fine print? It states that, since

Kalen doesn't have blood from both parents within the...whatever it's called...founder families, the only way he can be the sole ruler of the kingdom is to marry me, knock me up, and take my position because he's a man."

"I didn't know. I can't speak for Monty. I'm so sorry. I planned to tell you everything as soon as I could. If I went against them, they would have sent in an execution team to take me – and anyone standing in their way – out."

"What about my grandma?"

"Long story... but when I was a boy, I was sent to what you know now as Knox Academy. Her parents were trying to make a deal. Her twin brother had died and they needed a Rossi. Since she was a female and couldn't take part in The Order, I was sent when it was my turn. Basically, she was pissed. It's information she shouldn't have known, but in her brother's journal he told her everything. She built her own empire here and refuses to work with The Order. There's a lot more to it but that's the gist of it."

"I want to meet her."

"That isn't a good idea," he says, shaking his head.

"I'll take her," Smalls says, making his presence known.

"Jason…" My father warns.

"I promise, she is safe with me. I will even take her bodyguards."

My head snaps between my father and Smalls.

"Bodyguards?"

"You really didn't think those assholes would send you halfway across the globe after an attack on you, and not have you watched?"

My father looks as surprised as I am.

"Your little psycho friend made an impression on your grandmother, so she allowed some of The Order's men to keep watch over you. Ordinarily, they would have been taken out as soon as they hit Australian soil."

"Baxter?" I question and Smalls nods.

What the actual fuck is going on?! My head is swimming with information that I'm not yet processing. All I've taken from this is my grandmother is a badass gangster and didn't let a male dominated industry keep her from building an empire. This is a woman I need to meet.

"Amelie..." my father says.

"Yeah?"

"Do not talk about The Order. Your boyfriends can't save you if you do."

I nod in understanding. I follow Smalls out to his car and giggle. I may or may not have raided Chelsea's craft cupboard last night in a bout of anger. Childish? Yes. Funny as fuck? Hell yes.

I jump in the passenger seat as soon as he opens the door, angling the air vents upwards and away from me. He doesn't turn on the air straight away, he rolls the windows down to let out the hot air. We make it down the street and to a set of traffic lights before he leans over and turns the dial. I snort, trying to hold in my laugh, but it all happens so quickly. His face turns and is hit with a huge cloud of glitter. I clutch my stomach as tears roll down my face.

"What the fuck?!" he roars.

I compose myself as the asshole behind us honks his horn. Smalls ignores him and tries to dust the glitter off, making it worse as it sticks to the sweat on his face and hands.

"What the fuck, Amelie?!"

"So you are talking to me? I wasn't sure. I figured after your jealous bullshit and treating me like A-grade shit, that you must have been talking to someone else."

He proceeds to drive, giving up on trying to remove the glitter. He will be finding that in places men don't want glitter for weeks. I pull out my phone and snap a picture, uploading it straight to social media and tagging him in it with the caption *'There is a time and place for glitter...always and everywhere'*. That serves him right.

"I'm sorry, okay? I was a jealous asshole. You've always been mine in a way, and I liked that. I felt like what we had was slipping away and they were taking you away from me."

"You're right, you are an asshole. But we will always be us, just with a clearer line we won't cross. And no one will ever take me away from you. You are, and have always been, my best friend. I need you in my life. I couldn't live in a world where we were not friends, it would kill me. You're my rock."

"And how do your boyfriends feel about that?"

I shrug.

"Kalen is Kalen and thinks he's god's gift, so he is fine. Sawyer knows how much I care about you. Slate, I don't think has an opinion, and Onyx probably wants to murder you in your sleep."

"He can try..." Smalls mutters darkly. "Was glitter really necessary?"

I look over at him and laugh again.

"Yep."

"I hate you," he moans.

"No, you don't," I say as we pull into a huge ass mansion right on the lake. Hence why this area is called The Lakes.

"Shit, you guys live here?" He nods.

"So does your grandmother. And her housekeeper and housekeeper's daughter. Just wait until you see the daughter and Aadi together, she drives him crazy and it is bloody hilarious."

"I bet."

Once the security opens the gate, I gawk out the window. The lawns are mowed to perfection, the shrubs lining the fence are pruned to perfection, and she has a fucking massive ass fountain.

"Pretentious, much?" I snort when we pull up into a parking space and climb out of the car.

"Let's just say your grandmother has money, and she likes the finer things in life."

The door flies open and a curvy little Italian woman stands at the top of the stairs. I freeze. She almost looks identical to me, curly hair and all.

"Mia nipote!" she cries and rushes down the stairs with her arms open wide. Wrapping them tight around me, she speaks Italian in between obsessively kissing my face over and over.

"Come, let's feed you. You are way too skinny!" She then looks up at Smalls, who dwarfs both of us, and husky laughter falls from her lips. She hooks her arm in mine and walks us towards the house, Smalls trailing behind us. Inside we are greeted by a housekeeper who looks less than pleased that Smalls is covered in glitter; her nose scrunches, but she doesn't voice her opinion.

"Saide, this is my granddaughter Amelie. Could you set up brunch?" The housekeeper nods and informs my grandmother she has a call. Smalls is instructed to take me to the sitting room where we will be eating.

"Ho lee shit boi, what happened to you?" a girl around my age says, covering her mouth to stifle a laugh. She's wearing cargo pants that hang low on her hips, a crop top that shows off her impressive abs, and a hat covering her long chestnut coloured hair. "Looks like a unicorn shit all over you."

"Ha-ha, don't you have some cleaning to do or something?" Small's teases.

"Come upstairs with me and I will clean you, big boi," she flirts back. She seems to be teasing him too.

"Nope, I don't need another reason for Aadi to kill me."

"That wanker doesn't scare me," she scoffs.

"That wanker is my brother," I say. The girl stares at me for a moment and then the recognition slowly dawns on her face. Clearly, she's only now just recognising me, or noticing me.

"I'm sorry to hear that. I'm Bexley but you can call me Bex."

"Amelie," I say, taking her outstretched hand.

"Sorry about the wanker thing. I don't have a filter and words just come out, and before I know it, my foot's in my mouth."

"Don't sweat it, he is generally an ass but I have to love him."

She throws her arm around me and leads us further into the house. I try to take in everything around me but Bex moves us quickly and I only manage to get a glimpse of some impressive artwork on the walls.

"I see you have met Bex," my grandmother says.

"This grandchild seems way better than the other one. I vote you switch them out and send the other one packing."

"Get out of here girl, your mother could use some help."

"See ya round, get my number off the big guy." She winks at me as she strides out of the room. I look at Smalls and he gives me an 'I will tell you later' look.

"Boy, go and do some work while I talk to my granddaughter."

"Yes, ma'am." Smalls leaves the room, glitter falling on the floor as he goes. I chuckle.

"You're so grown up. I haven't seen you since you were so small. Before we get to know each other, I just want to say be careful of those men, they can all be snakes. My brother... well that's another story, but please be careful."

"I am, and I have some pretty awesome people watching my back."

She changes the subject and the food is brought in. We talk about my new life in England and she tells me all about her travels. She is very tight lipped about what she does here in Australia, even though she knows I have some idea. I'm grateful she doesn't push for any information about The Order, and I respect that by not digging about what she does. Two hours pass before Smalls waltzes back in, freshly showered and mostly sans glitter, though there are still random spots I can see shimmering and twinkling under the lights.

"Aadi called, we have to head back and play happy families now."

"We are a happy family, Smalls."

He smiles but doesn't reply.

After we say our goodbyes, my grandmother makes me promise to come and visit her again before I leave and to bring Kalen with me. I'm not so sure about that. Kalen in this big expensive house would be bad enough, but Kalen with taboo topics we're not meant to speak about? Downright dangerous if you ask me.

Smalls and I ride back to our house in comfortable silence. I'm grateful we made up; I hate when we fight. We will get past this stage, especially if I help him find a girl. Come to think of it, Katie was giving him some serious love eyes at the funeral. This might be something I need Kalen's help with. I'm terrible at the whole romance thing but he, while over the top, seems to understand it. I smile to myself as we drive, plans slowly beginning to take shape in my mind.

Amelie: I just found out something very interesting...

Message delivered

Baxter: So what if my middle names are Baudelaire Bojangles?! Get over it.

Message delivered

Amelie: OMFG!!! WTF?! Seriously?! That is hilarious! Really?! You're not winding me up?!

Message delivered

Baxter: Wait, what? That isn't what you know?

Message delivered

Amelie: We need to talk about that later, but it's not what I know...

Message delivered

Baxter: See, this is why I don't do feelings OR friendships! I was caught up in a girl and gave away my secret.

Message delivered

Amelie: Girl? Like an actual living breathing honest to god real life girl that you're interested in? Now THIS we need to talk about!!! However, I thought you might want to know that I just met my grandmother.

Message delivered

Baxter: I'll call you from a secure line.

Message delivered

Chapter Sixteen

Baxter

I spoke to Camilla while I waited for Amelie's burner phone to be delivered. She assured me it was a family catch up and not related to business, but I don't entirely trust the woman. She's lethal and ruthless. She gushed about how perfect Amelie is to take over The Order and how she may actually consider doing business with her. That just makes me more suspicious. She never truly got over being barred from joining The Order herself, so I don't buy her joy at Amelie's promotion. Sure, she's worked hard to keep tabs on Amelie for her 'safety' but what better way to infiltrate and control The Order through her familial connection to its new, young and impressionable leader.

There's no denying Amelie has mother issues – hell, who doesn't – and I don't really blame her for being desperate for love after everyone she's ever trusted has lied to her for her entire life. But finding out that Laura isn't her mum and suddenly discovering a new family with both the Kesslers and Camilla is bound to confuse and screw with the girl. I don't trust Camilla not to manipulate Amelie, and as intelligent as Amelie is, she's too emotional not to fall for it until it's too late.

I protect her because Camilla is paying me to, but the overwhelming *need* to protect her comes from somewhere else. I think I have to shield her from her family too, and unfortunately I think the best way to do that *is* to have her join and take over The Order, but for me to stay in it too.

Actively.

Which fucking sucks.

It took me a few hours to find a burner phone and have it delivered to Amelie, but once I had word she received it, I headed as far away from prying eyes as I could. This island is huge so I had no problem finding a quiet spot to call her.

"Hey, Batman," she says, answering on the first ring.

"Excited to hear from me?"

"Pfft in your dreams! It was you who had a phone hand delivered to me from the other side of the world."

"Yeah, yeah."

"What's so important that we need burner phones?" she asks hesitantly.

"The Order." I reply curtly. I'm tense. Nervous. Scared. "You didn't say anything, right?"

"Does no one trust me? I don't fancy a bullet between my eyes any time soon." She sounds pissed and I smirk to myself, wondering who else has told her to keep her mouth shut. I doubt it was Kalen – he's far too oblivious to anything other than a good time to note the danger of Amelie being in Camilla's presence.

"Also," I hesitate. I don't want this to blow up in my face, but it needs to be said. "Be careful around your grandmother. She might look like a gentle little old lady but she would sell her soul to the devil for a pack of cigarettes."

"I did hear about you two knowing each other. Is that something The Order knows about?"

"No!" I snap. "And you can't tell them! They would kill me for being a traitor. I agreed to work with her for your protection. She called and we made a deal. Someone like her owing me a favour could be beneficial in the future. Besides, she's not exactly someone you say no to."

"Calm your tits, I won't tell anyone. It will be our secret, and Aadi, Smalls, and my father."

"Fuuuck." I groan, hitting my forehead with my palm. This is a disaster. Two can keep a secret if one of them is dead, and she's only gone and told half of the bloody outback! "You know your father is in The Order, right? If he says anything…"

A million thoughts rush through my head. I can't wait, can't risk it. He needs to be taken care of. It's too dangerous not to. But…I can't kill him. Amelie would hate me, along with The Order sending a team after me. Shit. Going off grid was my original plan but this damn dark-haired girl with a smart mouth has made me question everything.

"I'll talk to my dad. He hates The Order as much as you do, so I'm sure he won't say anything if I ask him not to."

"You would do that for me?" I ask in disbelief. Why would she? I wouldn't if the roles were reversed. Although…the raven-haired beauty flashes in my mind and I wonder what I might be persuaded to do for her.

"That's what friends *do* for each other, Baxter. I worry about you sometimes. Were you dropped on your head as a baby? Left to be raised by a pack of wolves? I mean, friendship really isn't a hard concept to grasp."

"It is where I come from. It's better going it alone, no one can stab you in the back while you're not looking."

"Baxter…"

I can just imagine her shaking her head at me, but there's worry in her tone too.

"What is it?" I want to snap, but I force myself to sound…softer? Caring? I don't know. Just different somehow, like I'm inviting her to confide in me rather than demanding that she spills whatever it is that's bothering her.

"My grandmother made me promise to go back and visit her before I leave."

"So?" I frown. I don't see it being *that* much of an issue…yet.

"She said I have to take Kalen with me."

"Fuck." That's not okay. Not good.

"Who are you talking to? That better not be my nutsack of a brother." Kalen's voice filters down the line as our call gets interrupted. I may have ensured privacy for this call but it seems Amelie didn't think to do the same.

"I better leave you to it. I have a plane to catch anyway. I'll think about that last thing you just said but please don't do anything until you hear from me." I hang up before she starts to snoop about where I'm going.

I'll have time on the plane to come up with a plan to get Kalen out of meeting that woman. I don't think it would be in anyone's best interests for them to meet. No, my suspicions of what Camilla may be up to have now skyrocketed. From cautious paranoia to downright knowing she's up to something. I will get to the bottom of it and do whatever it takes to protect Amelie in the process.

Now it's time for me to head back home and go see said nutsack brother.

Amelie: So just to clarify...

Message delivered

Baxter: It's not that hard. Just stay away from Camilla until I can figure things out. And don't mention anything to anyone.

Message delivered

Amelie: Oh chill out, I'm not a moron. It's not like I posted it on Facebook or anything. Just Instagram. Selfies with my granny :)

Message delivered

Baxter: I know you're lying.

Message delivered

Amelie: Because you follow me on Insta? Stalker alert!

Message delivered

Baxter: No, because if you called Camilla granny on a public forum you wouldn't be breathing right now, blood or not.

Message delivered

Amelie: Touché. Or should I say touchy? Anyway, that wasn't what I wanted to clarify.

Message delivered

Baxter: Is it important? I'm busy.

Message delivered

Amelie: Just checking...your name is Baxter Baudelaire Bojangles Branson. What the actual fuck, Batman?!

Message delivered

Baxter: What?

Message delivered

Amelie: Well first, that takes alliteration to a whole new level. And Baudelaire has to be the most pompous name known to man. It's even more pretentious than Baxter Branson.

Message delivered

Baxter: Charles Baudelaire was a famous French poet I'll have you know. Besides, it's my father's and my grandfather's middle name too.

Message delivered

Amelie: I thought it sounded kinda girly. Besides, I just think of the Baudelaire orphans.

Message delivered

Baxter: ???

Message delivered

Amelie: Do you live under a rock?! Honestly. Let's move on.

Message delivered

Baxter: What now?

Message delivered

Amelie: One word: Bojangles?

Message delivered

Baxter: Do you have a point? I really am busy.

Message delivered

Amelie: You're named after a fictional character in a song?

Message delivered

Baxter: Bojangles wasn't fictional. He was a homeless guy that the singer met. And I happen to like that part of my name. It was the only part that my mother picked, and she secretly added it to my birth certificate without my father's permission. He was too busy to register my birth with her so she took advantage of that. It's the only thing of hers that I have left.

Message delivered

Amelie: Shit, I'm sorry. I didn't realise. You never talk about your family. Or yourself.

Message delivered

Amelie: Don't think this is going to stop me putting shit on you though...I mean, your damn initials are BJ for shit's sake! Lol!

Message delivered

Chapter Seventeen

Amelie

I snort thinking about Baxter's middle name. I mean, how awesome must his mother have been, to give her child the middle name Bojangles behind his father's back considering how pretentious the rest of his name is.

Bellowing laughter filters through my slightly ajar door and I decide it's time to get up from my afternoon nap. Chelsea had us at the beach all day and Kalen was so excitable the entire time. Making sandcastles, body boarding in the waves, chasing seagulls. There was never a dull moment.

I follow the laughter down the stairs and into the kitchen.

"Help me, it burns. It's so thick."

I rush towards the kitchen even faster. What the hell are they doing to Kalen? Rushing in, I Tom-Cruise-slide on the lino. Kalen has his head sideways under the kitchen sink, black gunk washing down the drain.

"What are you doing?" I demand, hands on my hips.

"Giving your boy toy a welcome to Australia."

Kalen surfaces, his face still scrunched up in disgust and

dripping with water.

"How do you eat that stuff? It tastes so bad!" he whimpers. My lips twitch.

Aadi and Smalls smile; Kalen's reaction has made their day.

"It's an acquired taste," Smalls says. "You did insist you were a *real man* and wanted a whole spoonful."

"You let him eat it off the spoon?"

They both nod.

"I can still taste it in my nose," Kalen whines.

"Less is more when it comes to Vegemite." I laugh. "Probably best to go brush your teeth."

He nods and runs out of the kitchen. Aadi and Smalls both look at each other and fall into hysterical laughter.

"What have you done?" I ask with dread.

"Just wait for it," Smalls replies.

"If he wants in with a Rossi, he needs a true lesson in sibling fun."

Oh god, he means our pranks.

Kalen's blood curdling scream fills the house. I shoot a quick disapproving look at Aadi and run up to the bathroom. Chelsea is close behind me.

Kalen screams and pleads for someone to help him. I push the bathroom door open. Someone is standing behind the door, and before I can get one step inside, Kalen shoots out of the room.

"It's behind the door! It tried to kill me!" he cries. I know Kalen's a massive drama queen and my brother's pranks are mostly harmless, but there's real fear etched on his face.

I step into the bathroom and look behind the door, expecting to find a spider or some kind of bug. Instead, I find a very tiny girl smiling back at me.

Kalen's issue with that? She's dressed like a clown.

"Katie?" I ask, and she nods.

"Have you killed it yet?!" Kalen cries.

I exit the bathroom and Katie follows behind me.

"No, it's just Katie."

"Get it away from me!" he cries.

Chelsea now has a sobbing Kalen in her arms, facing him away from the innocent looking girl dressed as a clown.

"Sorry. I lost a bet and this is what they made me do," Katie says, pulling off her clown wig. She walks back into the bathroom to get changed.

I turn back to see Kalen has composed himself a little. Chelsea points at Smalls and Aadi and gives them a 'follow me now' look. Chelsea may be a sweet woman but when she is mad, you will feel the wrath.

"I think I pissed myself a little," Kalen grumbles. His face still red from the terror my brother forced on him.

"I'm sorry about that, but if Aadi is pranking you it's a sign of endearment for us Rossis."

"So we are brothers now?" he asks hopefully.

"I wouldn't go that far, but you are growing on him."

"Like a damn fungus," Aadi groans, joining us back upstairs. "We're heading out in about half an hour if you're still up for it."

I stare up at my brother. "No more pranks."

"Scout's honour."

"You were no damn scout." I laugh and so does Aadi.

He doesn't wait for Kalen to respond to his invitation when the sound of a girl's voice catches his attention downstairs.

"You don't mind if I go?" Kalen asks.

"Of course not. Just take your phone, and if you need me, call.

If they're really giving you a welcome to the family it could go either way for you."

"I'm game. He pulled out the clown card early, so it can't get much worse than that."

I smile at him indulgently. He has no idea how much worse tonight could get for him. Knowing his luck, they will get him blind drunk, tie him up naked to a pole somewhere public and probably shave off his eyebrows too.

Katie slips out of the bathroom freshly showered. "I wasn't trying to eavesdrop, but Crystal and I are having a girls' night along with a few others if you want to join us?"

"Sounds fun. I'm in." I grin. While I never really did the girly thing before going to England, I miss Elsie, and some female company could be just what I need. Otherwise, without Kalen around to entertain, I'd probably spend the entire evening obsessing over Onyx and texting the others back home to find out how he *really* is.

"Awesome! I have to go talk to Jason but I'll wait for you."

I nod and she heads down the stairs.

Kalen pulls me into the spare room. "Want a quickie before we go out?" He waggles his brows at me in a completely over the top and not at all sexy gesture. I laugh.

"No way, the guys are just starting to like you."

"Good point, drunk sex later sounds better anyway."

I shake my head; he is incorrigible. Backing away, I poke my tongue out at him and slip through the door. He'll be down soon enough.

Walking down into the lounge, I could cut the tension with a knife. Smalls and Katie are sitting on the sofa next to each other. Smalls looks like a giant next to her. They're both staring at Aadi and Bex.

"Amelie," Bex says. "Tell your arrogant brother that it is totally acceptable to invite myself out with you girls. Everyone my age has balls and as much as I love balls, this testosterone is bullshit." Bex crosses her arms in front of her chest. Aadi is practically snarling at her across the room.

"Aad, it's fine. You don't mind her tagging along, do you Katie?"

I turn to Katie but she isn't paying attention. Smalls bumps his leg into hers.

"Huh? Oh, yeah, it's fine," she replies.

"Sweet! Let's get white girl wasted!" Bex sings, and Aadi groans.

❤ ❤ ❤

'Young dumb and broke' by Khalid pumps through the speakers as we all walk into the pub. Bex high fives a table of guys.

"Happy birthday," she says, winking at the guy on the end.

"Do you know him?" I ask.

"No. Should I?" She frowns back at me.

"You just told him happy birthday," Katie adds, sounding as puzzled as I feel.

"Well, I probably won't see him before his birthday so it's only polite to say it in advance." She shrugs like what she just said is a perfectly reasonable explanation and skips off towards the bar, high fiving the bartender when she gets there. The young guy leans over the bar and kisses her on the cheek. I hope she knows *that* guy.

"She's...interesting," Katie says. I nod. That's one way of

putting it, but I do like her.

We spot Crystal sitting near the pool tables and she waves us over.

"She sure is. I'll go order us some drinks. Any requests?" I ask.

"Nothing fruity," she replies before heading to join Crystal.

I make my way towards Bex, who is animatedly talking to the bartender still, laughing at whatever he just said.

"Ordered any drinks yet?" I ask. She looks back at me and smiles.

"Not yet, I was waiting for you. I wasn't sure what you wanted."

"Nothing fruity."

"Me either girl, my legs tend to fall open if I drink that girly shit." The bar tender grins lasciviously and nods. I know he's filed that information away for later. I see fruity girly drinks in Bex's future if the bartender has anything to say about it.

"Can I get eight tequila shots and a jug of Jack? Four cups, please."

We wait while the drinks are being made. I look back over at Katie and think how she really would make a good girlfriend for Smalls. They'd look super cute together and she's so much nicer than skank face Sarah.

"You hot for her?" Bex asks, bumping my shoulder.

"Me? No, I have four boyfriends. They're hot, but a handful. Don't need any more."

"Four?! We have to talk about this, but first what's the deal with the girl?"

"I was thinking of setting her up with Smalls."

"Jason? It would make it hard for sixty niners though."

I snort. This chick really just says the first thing that comes to mind. The bartender slides a tray towards Bex and she passes the cash to him.

"Keep the change, Nick."

"I kind of thought that you and Jason were a thing. He always talks about you. I've been curious to meet you. He holds you on this pedestal, and I reckon it will be pretty impossible for anyone to measure up to that."

"We've sorted it out, we're both moving on," I say dismissively. I like Bex, but I don't want to get into that whole mess with her. My relationship with Smalls is complicated enough without spilling my secrets to a virtual stranger.

We reach the table and Bex introduces herself to Crystal and takes a seat after letting me slide in ahead of her.

"So, did Amelie tell you she has four boyfriends?" Bex announces to the table. Crystal's mouth makes an O shape and Katie looks indifferent; clearly she already knows, someone has filled her in. Probably Smalls. I wonder how that conversation went down.

'Bad things' by Camila Cabello and MGK catches Bex's attention, taking the focus off me and my four boyfriends.

"Fuck, I love MGK. He is so damn hot. He kinda reminds me of your brother."

"My brother?" I scoff. "They look nothing alike."

"I mean, if he dyed his hair and lost the baby fat on his face," she jokes. Aadi has a square jaw, whereas MGK doesn't.

"Can we go back to the four boyfriends?" Crystal asks. "Who and how does that work? That blonde hottie is fine as hell and now you're telling me there are three more?"

"Yep. They're all sorta adopted brothers. Though two of them are actual brothers. Twins actually," I reply happily.

"Ohmygod!" Crystal's eyes are like saucers at my declaration.

"Did you have a twin sandwich yet?" Bex asks. I can't keep the grin from my face. "Have you done it with all four of them? You know, at the same time?"

"Wouldn't that be weird?" I counter, frowning. I mean, it's not like I've *never* thought about it, but only in a passing fantasy kind of way.

"Fuck no!" Bex exclaims. "You have to do it!"

We spend the next few hours dancing, drinking and talking – mainly about my guys – and I run them through everything, minus The Order of the Sneezes. I also try to drop as many hints as I can to Katie about Smalls, but she acts as if she doesn't know what I'm talking about. I still see the slight blush every time I mention him though. Bex manages to talk about Aadi *way* more than someone should when they allegedly hate them.

By the time one in the morning rolls around we're all extremely drunk. When Crystal vomits on the dance floor we decided to call it a night. How she still managed to pick up and leave with a guy after that blows my mind.

Bex, Katie and I walk to the taxi rank. Usually they all line up here but tonight there's some event happening so the last taxi left already. We debate waiting.

"Walking would be faster," Katie points out.

"No way," I slur. 'If I walk anywhere alone, I'll be murdered. My brother isn't exactly a nice guy when it comes to my safety and the guys…" Talking of the guys, I get a brain fart. I have security. Surely they have to be around here somewhere?

"Come out, come out, wherever you are," I yell in my drunken state.

"Who are you yelling at?" Bex demands. "You'll attract the

crazy people."

"She *is* the crazy people!" Katie adds with a giggle.

"I know you're there! I will strip off naked and walk home. While I make a phone call to Baxter. I'm calling now." I mention Baxter because if these guys work for The Order, then Baxter is the name to drop.

A tall man slips out of the shadows holding a walkie talkie.

"Don't come any closer! I know kung fooooooo and I'm not afraid to use it!" Bex cries, holding herself up in some kind of pose that is supposed to be threatening but just looks ridiculous. She kinda reminds me of a female Kalen, only less annoying. I laugh until my stomach hurts, tears streaming down my face.

"Calm down, kung fu panda, he's my security."

"You have security?! Why? Are you famous?" Katie shriek-slurs and falls into Bex's arms.

A car pulls up to the curb beside us and Security One runs around and opens the door. Bex attempts to contort Katie's body and shove her into the car.

"Holy fuck, this is more work than trying to shove a soft cock into a pussy."

"Meow," Katie purrs.

Bex and I cry with laughter as I help her push Katie into the car and buckle her in. With absolutely no help whatsoever from the security guy. I huff. Jasper and Frost would have helped.

"Miss Rossi, we have been instructed to take you home first."

"Aye aye, captain!" Bex salutes.

As we drive home Katie snores and Bex chats up the security – who really do try their best not to engage with her, but she makes it impossible. I laugh almost the entire way back to the house. I don't realise we've pulled up out the front of Dad's house until Aadi runs over to the car.

"A little help please?" he asks, pointing towards his car. His friend Paddy looks horrified in the front seat.

I slide from the car and Aadi slides in. "What do you think you're doing, perv?" Bex snaps.

"Pfft, as if I would perv on your manly ass."

"Manly?! You could bounce coins off this baby!" she snarls as the car pulls away.

I jog over to Paddy's car and open the back door. Kalen is naked and sprawled across the entire seat.

"Where are his clothes?" I ask Paddy. He looks at me and shrugs.

"Kalen, it's time for bed."

"No," he whines. "I wanna dance."

He starts humming under his breath and it takes me a moment to figure out the tune.

"Is that...are you singing...Ghostbusters?"

"WHO YA GONNA WHATSAPP?!"

"This is *not* how the song goes, Kalen."

"MY SISTER!" he continues to scream-sing at me oblivious to the time, his nakedness, or the danger of waking the street. I need to get him quiet and inside. Quickly.

"Hey, Kalen? What about that drunken sex I was promised?"

Kalen suddenly springs up out of his seat and slides out of the car with the grace of a ballerina.

"You didn't hear a thing," I warn Paddy.

"Hear what?"

I grin and nod, and he reverses the car out of the driveway as soon as I push the back door closed.

"Did you know Aus is like the hunger games?" Kalen whines

in my ear. He's trying to be quiet but he's still kinda loud.

"Okay," I say to placate him, hauling his ass through the house.

"Just tonight there were kangaroos hop-hop-hopping across the road in front of cars and they were buff…" I shake my head in amusement at him. Only Kalen could find a kangaroo buff.

"And the mozzies, oh dear god the mozzies! Amelie, why didn't you warn me?! Those bastards stole my blood." I look at him more closely and see the welts on his arms, angry and red. "And did you know you have ants that bite your nuts? I don't even know if I can have kids now. I can't feel my left nut. That was my favourite nut! Now it's broken," he finishes pitifully.

"Kalen—"

"And what sort of place has spiders that spin webs straight after you walk past them so when you turn around…BAM! You have that hairy fucker stuck between your face and its web? I can still taste it. And then there's owls that dive bomb your car! I used to like owls. Hedwig! Wise old Owl in Winnie the Pooh! The Owl and the Pussycat. Owl Brown!" He's practically crying now, randomly screaming famous owl names out at me.

"Kalen!" I hiss. "You need to shut the fuck up!"

"Where's the deadly mist? That's all that's missing."

Kalen finally stops ranting when I get him up the stairs. I push my door open and Kalen stumbles inside. We've slept apart to respect Chelsea's wishes, but tonight I plan to sleep in his arms. I just need it.

I manage to help him over to the bed and pull the covers back. He pulls me down with him and we both fall onto the bed. I give him a quick peck on the lips

"Did you know your brother is a criminal?" he whispers

conspiratorially to me.

"Yeah, I had an idea. No more so than you and your brothers." I smirk.

"Touché," he says, rolling me over so that we're spooning. "So how about that drunken sex?"

I laugh and Kalen takes that as a go ahead to pull off my pants.

"Kalen stop! I just wanna snuggle." I try to insist.

"Shush. It's total bullshit how little frolicking I get to do. I was made for frolicking! Let me show you how frolicky I can be."

"Kalen—"

He chastises me and tells me to keep quiet. When I try to stop him, he puts a pillow over my head to try to muffle out the noises I'm making. As his head descends between my thighs, I give up fighting him on this. Fucking hell. Drunk Kalen is damn good with his tongue.

Amelie: Almost home time, bet you can't wait to see me.

Message delivered

Baxter: You bet wrong.

Message delivered

Amelie: Liar, liar, pants on fire.

Message delivered

Amelie: Well I can't wait to see you. Kalen is driving me nuts. I need to spend time with someone levelheaded.

Message delivered

Baxter: And you think that I'm levelheaded?

Message delivered

Amelie: More so than Kalen. He thinks Australia has its own version of the hunger games.

Message delivered

Baxter: Can you blame him? You have spiders the size of dinner plates!

Message delivered

Amelie: Are you afraid of spiders, Batman?

Message delivered

Baxter: Piss off, I'm not afraid of anything.

Message delivered

Amelie: Except feelings.

Message delivered

Baxter: Sorry, who am I speaking to again?

Message delivered

Amelie: Your BFF. If you're lucky we can make each other friendship bracelets.

Message delivered

Baxter: *Insert middle finger emoji*

Message delivered

Chapter Eighteen

Baxter

Stepping off the curb at the airport, I wait for my driver to open the door. As much as I dread my next stop, it needs to be done. Camilla called again before I left and made it clear that she will be actively getting to know her granddaughter but that doesn't sit well with me. She lived so close to Amelie her whole life, but never bothered with her? It's only now that she is joining The Order that Camilla wants her around.

How she even knows that Amelie passed initiation or even ran in the contest...well, it means there is a mole among us. I may have worked with her to keep Amelie safe, but I would never open my mouth about the details of what was happening. Even I couldn't hide from the ones they send to take you out.

I make a call to Frost and get the run down on some information I asked him to find me. He also informs me that Onyx is staying at Sawyer's house. I don't blame him, I wouldn't stay with that horrid woman Monty calls a fiancée. Her and Cordelia would be in the running for biggest cunt of the year. I fucking despise them both. I can't wait to help Amelie take revenge on

Laura. One day I might even get to deal with Cordelia too.

I have to keep myself busy; a certain dark-haired beauty keeps entering my thoughts. I have never been infatuated with anyone or anything like this before. Not since...well, the two people who landed me in Knox in the first place, but those thoughts get firmly locked down. Like always.

As Amelie would say, it has thrown me for a loop. What has Raven done to me? This new pansy-ass version of Baxter Branson is pathetic. I should just off myself now. It's all downhill from here at this point. What's next? Two point five kids, a golden lab called Buddy and a white picket fence? Kill me now.

Only, I can totally see that raven haired beauty and I making amazing babies together. And I'd make sure we had a hell of a lot of fun making them.

We pull up at Sawyer's house and my driver lets me out.

"Take my things home, I have a friend bringing my bike."

That's a lie. I don't let anyone touch my bike. Ever. I've used wire cutters to dismember fingers over smaller infractions. Except Amelie. She touches the damn bike. I also don't have any friends. Except Amelie. But she's still halfway across the world. And I don't like that either. It's irrelevant; I can find my own way home, I don't want a damn driver hanging around for this.

"What are you doing here?" Onyx snaps when he opens the door in just a towel. Looking him up and down, objectively, I try to see what Amelie might see in him, but I just can't.

"You knew I was coming, dick," I snap back. Maybe not now, or here to the house, but that's on him for assuming otherwise. "We need to talk and now is as good a time as any."

"Hurry your ass inside, it's cold and my brothers will be back in an hour."

He doesn't wait for me or offer to hang up my coat, not that I expected him to. I shut the door and throw my coat over the armchair, along with my gloves.

Onyx reappears in a pair of sweats. "Coffee?"

"Tea, if you have it."

He mumbles something about Sawyer but puts the kettle on and potters around the kitchen, while I sit in silence until he is done and places the steaming mug in front of me.

"So, what was so important that you thought we could have a civil conversation and not kill each other?"

"Amelie's safety," I state.

Onyx stares at me, waiting for me to elaborate as I take a sip of my tea. It tastes like shit. He doesn't understand tea at all but I refrain from pulling a face. Tea is an art form and Onyx is an uncouth yob.

"Camilla is up to something and I want your help finding out why."

"Are you trying to steal my girl?" Onyx asks suddenly, acting as though I never even spoke. I laugh.

I would one hundred percent have fucked her if she had wanted it. Now we are so far into the friend zone my dick is safely tucked away in my trousers. He's practically fucking turtling.

"No. Believe it or not, Amelie is my friend. For no ulterior motive. Shocking, I know. I didn't believe it either at first."

"Fine, what do you know?"

I run through everything, even admitting to working for Camilla to keep Amelie safe. Onyx agrees he would have done the same thing, so I doubt there's a hit on my head yet.

It's too late for Amelie to walk away now, it would disrespect the board, especially the ones backing her. So we need a solid plan to deal with this. Onyx and I discuss our options but ultimately we agree that we're going to have to work together on this.

Amelie isn't stupid. She would have her doubts as to why Camilla hasn't fought harder to be in her life, but if we come out and forbid her from getting to know her grandmother, she will do everything in her power to be on Camilla's side. I'm sure that is what the old bat wants.

I'm struggling to understand what it is that Camilla does want. She was also rejected for being a woman, and that would have hurt her pride, so she wouldn't just be happy for Amelie. There has to be more...something we don't know about.

Being Amelie's blood?

Total world domination springs to mind.

Baxter: Be careful, I have a gut feeling.

Message delivered

Amelie: It's probably diarrhoea, pack a spare pair of undies!

Message delivered

Baxter: I'm being serious.

Message delivered

Amelie: When are you not? Maybe that's why you have the shits.

Message delivered

Baxter: I'm going to spend the rest of my life protecting your ass.

Message delivered

Amelie: #LifeGoals

Message delivered

Baxter: I give up, you're a lost cause.

Message delivered

Amelie: See you soon Batman bestie.

Message delivered

Baxter: I hate you.

Message delivered

Amelie: Lies.

Message delivered

Chapter Nineteen

Amelie

I can't believe how quickly our time here has gone and that it's almost time to head home. Shit, better not call it home around Aadi, they'll blow a fuse. Smalls might be accepting of my decision to stay in the UK when everything is over, but I don't think Aadi ever will be.

It's been an amazing trip but seeing the boys moving on with their life and discovering that they're no longer in our family home, waiting for my return, has given me the boost I needed. I've been on the fence, worrying about committing to The Order and debating what to do after my time at Knox is over. Now I know that whatever happens, I no longer feel obliged to come back here for someone else. I can at least choose what *I* want for once.

I slip out of bed and take a shower before anyone else wakes up. It's sweet really that Aadi and Smalls came home to play happy families while I was here, but I'd rather have hot water. It'll be my last chance for a couple of days until we get home. Kalen fucked up the flights and we have a stupid layover somewhere, and all I can think is I just want to get home to the rest of my guys. Don't get me wrong, being here with Kalen has been amazing, but nearly two weeks away with just him has me about ready to cry. I need some adult company. I miss Sawyer's wisdom, Slate's calming presence, Onyx's snark. God I miss them so much. I've been so busy making sure Kalen had a good time, that it's just hitting me now how much I need to reconnect with the others. Especially Onyx. I need to see that he's okay to believe it.

I gently tap on Kalen's door as I make my way back to my room to get dressed. I need to finish packing but I want to check on him first. A groan of pain comes from within, so I open the door without waiting for an invite.

"Are you okay?" I ask with amusement lacing my voice. I don't have any sympathy for him.

"I'm dying. Go away. Call my family to fly out here for my funeral."

Yesterday was Easter, and while it's not usually such a big deal for us, Chelsea – surprise, surprise – went all out to make Kalen feel 'at home'. We had a massive Easter egg hunt all around the neighbourhood, played games, and had another barbecued feast fit for a king. Only Kalen discovered that he loves Aussie chocolate and ate the lot in one go.

As in, all of his chocolate. Then Smalls and Aadi thought it would be funny to give the kid with ADHD theirs too. He stole mine in a sugar frenzy and when he later crashed from the high, Chelsea took pity on his huge puppy dog eyes and shared hers with him too. Only my dad was safe from Kalen's theft and that's because he always has beer instead of chocolate and Kalen doesn't really like the stuff all that much.

"Oh Kalen, stop being melodramatic. I told you not to eat so much chocolate."

"But it tastes sooooo good," he whines.

"Zero sympathy. Get your lazy ass up and shower before the boys steal all the hot water. They'll do it just to mess with you, you know. And then pack all your crap. We have stuff to do today before we catch our flight."

"What stuff? I just wanna chill."

"You can chill on the flight. We have to go say bye to my grandmother."

At my words, Kalen sits bolt upright in bed, wincing and turning a funny shade of green from the sudden movement. He groans again.

"Grandmother? How is it possible that I've been here a fortnight with you, and have met every relative, friend and hanger-on in the damn state, and you're only just *now* mentioning a grandma?!"

"It's a long story."

"I sense dirt. And I really want the juicy details, but I feel sick—"

"Go! Get to the bathroom then! If you throw up, Chelsea will make you clean it up yourself."

"That's savage."

"If it's self-inflicted, you're fair game."

"Chelsea loves me, she wouldn't do that to me."

"She would and she will. Puke is a hard limit for her."

"But I'm poorly!"

"Kalen, you have a damn bellyache from eating too much sugar. Suck it the fuck up, and shut up!" I snap, losing my patience with him.

"Fine." He huffs, flinging back the covers and climbing from the bed. He's completely naked.

"Kalen!" I hiss. "You can't sleep naked in a guest bed!"

"Ooops, bit late for that." He glances down at the pile of discarded clothes he's dumped on the floor. "Can you get me my pants? I can't bend down."

"For fuck's sake!"

I do it though. Anything for an easy life. Crouching on the floor in my towel, I grab Kalen's shorts and pass them to him.

"You do it, if I bend down I'll puke!"

Sighing, I gather up the material and tap the top of his foot for him to lift. He places his hands on the top of my head for balance and moans loudly as he wobbles.

"What the fuck!?" I jump at the sound of an angry voice behind me and spin to see Aadi standing in the doorway. "What the fuck are you doing to my sister?!"

"She's putting my pants on. Why?" Kalen asks, confused. I snigger. He must really be feeling unwell if he can't see how this looks. In fact, I would have expected him to be thrusting his monster cock in my face. It's too good an opportunity to miss.

Ignoring Aadi, I tap Kalen's other foot and help guide it through the leg hole. Done, I guide the shorts up his legs and around his waist.

"There you go," I say, standing. "You can do them up yourself."

"Thanks, sis," he whimpers.

"She's not your damn sister, you sick fuck!" Aadi seethes.

"Okay, okay, enough. Aadi, get out. Kalen, go for a damn shower."

I leave them both and stomp back along the hallway to my own room. Once I'm dried and dressed, I hastily throw the rest of my stuff into my suitcase. There's not much to take back; I left most of my things here, not needing them in the dead of winter back in England. I'm just checking in on Elsie and the guys back home when there's a knock at my door.

Kalen pokes his head around, eyes lighting up when he sees my half empty suitcase lying open on the bed.

"Oh good! Have you finished packing?"

"Pretty much, why?"

"My case is full. Can I put some stuff in yours?"

"Sure. So long as it's not drugs or anything that's going to get me stopped by security." I laugh.

"I did that to Onyx once. He beat me so bad I'd never do it again," Kalen says seriously. I can only imagine.

"Fine. Get in here. But if I'm over the weight limit, you're damn well paying for it!"

"No problem, sis!"

"Not your damn sister, Kalen," I sigh, like a broken record stuck on repeat. Kalen just gives me a quick peck on the cheek before dumping the armful of crap he's holding down into my case in a heap. It's a total mess, but I'm not exactly Marie Kondo when it comes to packing and folding anyway so I don't whinge at him.

"What is all this crap?" I frown, staring at a wooden boomerang that's somehow got tangled around my pants.

"Souvenirs. Presents. Authentic Aussie momentos. You know. Stuff." Kalen shrugs. I finger the inflatable life sized kangaroo and raise a brow at him. "It's for Onyx."

I shake my head and decide it's best not to ask.

"Listen, are you ready? We have to go see—"

"Your grandma! Of course I'm ready! I can't believe you've

hidden her away from me this whole time. Old people *love* me! We're going to be besties, bonding over knitting and blue rinses."

I snort at the visual image of the poised and elegant, yet tiny and terrifying lady I met a few days ago doing knitting while having a blue tint put on her hair and getting a perm. Kalen's in for a rude awakening if he's expecting my grandmother to be a frail little old lady. Even without Baxter's insight, I could tell right away that she isn't someone to mess with.

"Mmm-hmm," I reply noncommittally. "Since when have you had a blue rinse?"

"One year I convinced Slate to dress as a Samurai warrior for Halloween, but didn't tell him I was ordering him the Mulan costume. His revenge was to dye my hair blue. I looked like a freaking Smurf for weeks."

"I would have loved to have seen that." I laugh.

"I'm sure we can dig out the pictures. Slate rocked a kimono."

We're interrupted by Smalls poking his head around the door.

"You ready, kid? Car's here to take you to Camilla's and then straight on to the airport."

I glance over my shoulder at Kalen who is sitting on my case in a desperate attempt to close it. Jesus, how much crap has he been buying on those trips out with Chelsea? I shake my head in exasperation at him and give Smalls a smile.

"Ready as I'll ever be."

I leave Kalen and Smalls to get the bags and head downstairs to say goodbye to my dad and Chelsea. Aadi too if he's calmed down enough to stop being an ass and come say goodbye to me.

In the kitchen, everyone assembles and I say goodbye to them all. It's a lot less painful than last time because I'm at peace with my decisions now.

We head out and Kalen plugs in, before laying his head in my lap and groaning. I run my fingers through his hair, grateful once again that it's growing back. I loved his hair when it was longer. Not everyone can pull off shoulder length hair, but Kalen with his carefree attitude and good looks can pull off anything.

"Why did you cut your hair?" I whisper to him, curious.

"Didn't."

"Kalen—" Why is he lying to me?

"Branson did it. He beat the crap out of us in your honour or some shit. Knew cutting my hair would hurt worse than any punches he could throw."

I blink in surprise at that snippet of information. I recall Baxter's split knuckles and the guys' injuries but I never considered Kalen's hair being connected to that event. I also didn't really understand why Baxter would do that.

After that, the drive is quiet and as we pull into Camilla's driveway I notice it's very different to the other day. This time, the front door is guarded by some skeezy looking gang bangers and goosebumps rise on my arms. Surely this isn't a trap?

Kalen sits up beside me, squeezing my hand and giving me a look of concern.

"Your granny isn't a sweet little old lady, is she?"

"No, Kalen."

"Is this safe?"

I hesitate. I really want to say yes, but I don't know this woman at all. Just because she used some Italian terms of endearment and hugged me, doesn't mean she cares for me.

I consider texting Baxter, but what can he do from the other side of the world? Maybe I should ring Smalls or Aadi. My father's earlier warning rings in my head. I shouldn't have brought Kalen here.

Shit. The gates close behind us and I realise it's too late to leave.

As the car pulls to a stop at the top of the driveway, the front door opens and my 'sweet little old lady' grandmother steps out. She looks taller than last time. She's dressed impeccably, head to toe in black, with a diamond necklace glinting at her throat.

She smiles warmly at me but I can't help but feel that it doesn't reach her eyes. The driver gets out and opens the car door for me. I slide out and am about to greet her when she turns to speak to someone just inside the house.

"Amelie?" Kalen asks. In my peripheral vision I see him turn to face me but I can't tear my eyes away from the newcomer as she steps out into the light. "Do you know who that is?"

The newcomer looks exactly like she did in the photographs I once saw. She hasn't aged at all. I can't believe that when I glanced over the images, I thought I didn't recognise her. Now I feel like I could be staring in a mirror. Only one that shows my future in twenty years' time maybe.

"Amelie?" Kalen asks when I fail to respond. "Do you know this woman?"

"Fuck," I manage to croak out. "Yeah, I do."

"Is that..." I turn to Kalen and his eyes are saucers, flirting back and forth between me and the woman standing beside my grandmother. "Is she...?"

"My real mother?" I croak out in disbelief as I stare at the 'dead' woman in front of me.

"Yeah?"

"Fuck. Yeah. She is."

"Fuck."
"Yeah."

Books by Crystal North and Jaye Pratt

F*ck You: Knox Academy Term 1

F*ck off: Knox Academy Term 2

F*ck Yeah: Knox Academy Term 2.5 Easter Break

F*ck Her: Knox Academy Term 3 (coming soon)

Books by Crystal North

Vengeance

Atonement

Retribution (coming soon)

Jasmine Spell Library

Frozen in time

Bearing the Curse

Torture: A halloween anthology

Fractured Remains

Her Christmas Wish

Bosses Brat

Trick or Treat

About the Author

Crystal North

Crystal North is a UK born and raised author, who lives many secret lives. She started her writing journey back in May 2019 when on maternity leave from teaching, and has never looked back since. During her time as an author, Crystal had planned to keep her writing a secret, however that all changed when she was outed on her last day at work! She also quit teaching to spend more time writing / raising her little one, choosing to work part time in education instead.

Crystal, when she's not doing all of the crazy listed above, loves long hot bubble baths with a good book, candles and crystals. She loves the outdoors, travel, unfinished stories, swearing too much, and plotting who she would include in her harem. The list is now so long she feels she might have to hold auditions. Luckily, she has a very understanding husband that she shares her home with in the beautiful Devonshire countryside, along with their miracle son (who is secretly named after some of her book boyfriends) and their Miniature Schnauzer fur baby.

Jaye Pratt

Jaye Pratt was born in Frankston Victoria and as a young child, she moved to sunny Queensland. Jaye is a wife and mother to six children. While raising her children for the last eighteen years, she decided she wanted to pursue her love of writing, which started with her love of reading. It is the one thing that became her break and escape of insanity of a large family. Jaye loves being a full-time mother, watching her children grow and enjoying every minute of it.

Acknowledgements

We acknowledge the fact we have not killed each other yet.

Printed in Great Britain
by Amazon